**OTHER NOVELS BY KEVIN HENKES**

*Olive's Ocean*

*The Birthday Room*

*Sun & Spoon*

*Protecting Marie*

*Words of Stone*

*The Zebra Wall*

*Two Under Par*

*Return to Sender*

# KEVIN HENKES

## BIRD LAKE MOON

GREENWILLOW BOOKS

*An Imprint of* HarperCollins*Publishers*

Book design by Paul Zakris. This book is printed on acid-free paper. Library of Congress
Cataloging-in-Publication Data. Henkes, Kevin. Bird Lake moon / by Kevin Henkes.   p. cm.
"Greenwillow Books." Summary: Twelve-year-old Mitch and his mother are spending the summer
with his grandparents at Bird Lake after his parents separate, and ten-year-old Spencer and his
family have returned to the lake where Spencer's older brother drowned long ago, and as
the boys become friends and spend time together, each of them begins to heal.
ISBN 978-0-06-147076-9 (trade bdg.) — ISBN 978-0-06-147078-3 (lib. bdg.)
[1. Divorce—Fiction. 2. Grief—Fiction. 3. Lakes—Fiction. 4. Friendship—Fiction.
5. Family life—Wisconsin—Fiction. 6. Wisconsin—Fiction.]  I. Title.
PZ7.H389Bir 2008  [Fic]—dc22  2007036564
First Edition 10 9 8 7 6 5 4 3 2 1
Greenwillow Books

For Susan

# 1 ● MITCH

Mitch Sinclair was slowly taking over the house, staking his claim. He had just finished carving his initials into the underside of the wooden porch railing, which was his boldest move so far. The other things he had done had required much less courage. He had swept the front stoop with his grandmother's broom. He had cleaned the decaying leaves and the puddle of murky water out of the birdbath in the side yard and filled it with fresh water. He had spat on the huge rotting tree stump at the corner of the lot each day for the past week, marking the territory as his. And he had taken to crawling under the screened back porch during the hot afternoons; he'd lean against the brick foundation in the cool shade, imagining a different life, if, as his mother had said, their old life was over. Forever.

Although he'd seen the house many times while visiting his grandparents, Mitch had never paid much attention to it before. The house was vacant. It was old and plain—white clapboard with dark green trim—and had been neglected for quite a while, so that all its lines, angles, and corners were softened like the edges on a well-used bar of soap. The windows were curtained, keeping the interior hidden. However, the curtains covering the small oval window on the back door were parted slightly, offering a glimpse of a sparsely furnished, shadowy corner of a room. That's all. With some hesitancy, Mitch had tried to open the door, turning the loose knob gently at first, then rattling it harder and harder. The door wouldn't budge. The front door was locked as well. Mitch's grandparents' house stood a short distance from the vacant one. The two yards were separated by a row of scraggly lilac bushes and clumps of seashells that reminded Mitch of crushed bones.

Both yards sloped down to Bird Lake. Mitch went swimming nearly every day; he lived in his bathing suit. There were more people around because it was summer, and yet it was quiet. A sleepy, sleepy place, Mitch's grandfather called it. When Mitch made a casual observation at dinner one night—breaking the dreadful silence—about the lack of potential friends, his grandmother said crisply that she liked having as few children around as possible. She quickly added that she didn't mean him, of course. But Mitch hadn't been so sure.

Mitch ran his finger over his initials. M.S. His father's initials were W.S. Wade Sinclair. Turn an M upside down and you get a W, thought Mitch. We're the same. It was an idle thought, but it caused a burning knot to form in his stomach. "We're not the same at all," Mitch whispered. And we never will be. At the moment, Mitch hated his father, hated him and yet longed to see him so badly tears pricked his eyes. He thought he could destroy this empty little house right now with his bare hands, he was that upset. But he wanted this house. He wanted it for himself and for his mother. To live in.

Mitch rubbed his finger over his initials again. "Ouch," he said. A splinter. A big one. But not big enough to pick out without a tweezers or a needle. He retreated to his spot under the porch and settled in. He hadn't asked his grandparents yet what they knew about the house, because he didn't want an answer that would disappoint him. Maybe he'd ask today. He dozed off in the still, hazy afternoon, blaming his father for everything wrong in the world, including his aching finger.

Sometimes he wished his father had simply vanished. That would have been easier to deal with. Then he could make up any story he wanted to explain his father's absence. Or he could honestly say that he didn't know where his father was or why he had disappeared. And if he had vanished, there would be the possibility that, at any moment, he'd return. There he'd be, suddenly—hunched at the sink, humming, scrubbing a frying pan, a dish towel slung over his shoulder. A familiar pose. Everything back in its proper place, the way it was meant to be.

He even wondered if death would be better than the truth. An honorable death. If his father were killed trying to stop a robbery at a gas station . . . something like that. A car accident would be okay, too, if it were someone else's fault or caused by a surprise storm.

But the truth was worse. The truth was that two and a half weeks ago, his father hadn't come home from work. He had called that night to say that he was going to live with someone else, a woman from his office.

Mitch hated thinking of that night—his mother pressing apologies upon him, and then her silence and the way she kept hugging him, her shoulder bending his nose back until he had to squirm away. He'd felt as if he were nobody's child.

The following morning, his father made a couple of phone calls to Mitch that left him more confused than ever, and left him with more questions than answers.

As that day passed, and the next, Mitch's sadness grew; it became a rock inside him, pulling him down. He carried the sadness everywhere, morning, noon, and night. It hurt to breathe. And then, after three days of looking at each other with mutual uncertainty, Mitch and his mother packed up their most necessary possessions and drove to Mitch's grandparents' house on Bird Lake. "I can't live here anymore," Mitch's mother had said as she stuffed clothes into duffle bags. "We don't belong here, now."

She told him they'd come back sometime during the summer to straighten things out and to pick up whatever they might have forgotten. He told her about a new movie he'd heard of, not because he really cared about this, but because it was a way to keep her from saying things that made him more uneasy than he already was. At one point during their conversation, her voice cracked and she had to turn away for a moment before she began talking again.

She circled back to the same topic. "We couldn't afford to stay here if we wanted to, anyway," she said. "Not on a teachers' aide's salary."

It was June. School had just ended for the year, which made the situation easier for both of them.

"We can look at the bright side," said his mother, as they headed southeast out of Madison. But she never said what the bright side was.

Depending on traffic, it was about a two-hour drive to Bird Lake. They took the back roads, curving through small towns and past cornfields and new subdivisions. For most of the trip, the music on the radio was the only sound in the car. The harsh sunlight had volume and weight, and added to the general weariness Mitch felt.

"Will Dad know where to reach us?" Mitch asked, looking out at a particularly bucolic farm. He imagined the farm family: one trustworthy farm father, one reliable farm mother, one strong farm son. Everyone perfect and happy. "Did you tell him we'll be at Papa Carl and Cherry's?"

"Of course I told him," said his mother. "I left a message at work."

"What if he doesn't get the message?"

No answer.

"Will he call us?"

After a long pause, she said, "Yes. I don't know. Yes."

"This is just temporary, right? I mean, we'll move back to Madison before school starts in the fall."

This time her response was a shrug and a sigh. And then she made a high, tiny noise like the cry of a small bird. Her hands trembled slightly on the steering wheel.

His mother was usually calm, constant, consistent. She had become a different person. Someone he didn't know. And his father—now he couldn't believe anything he had ever believed about his father.

He really was nobody's child.

Mitch's maternal grandparents—Papa Carl and Cherry—took them in like mother bears welcoming home their long-lost cubs. At least, that's the way it felt to Mitch. There were freshly baked chocolate-chip cookies from Cherry and gifts of dollar bills concealed in hearty handshakes from Papa Carl and hugs from both of them. There were soothing refrains, some directed at Mitch and some overheard: "Of course you can stay," "What are families for?" "It's not your fault, Mr. Mitch. How could it be your fault?"

But before a full week had passed, a shift occurred. Arguments between Mitch's mother and grandmother leaked out from behind closed doors. And doors were slammed. Cherry sighed a bit too loudly and too often, her pleated face working like a mechanical toy, her chest heaving. And Papa Carl went off alone—fishing or running errands in his truck. He'd disappear for hours. Mitch longed to go with him but felt overcome by his growing shyness and was reluctant to ask. One afternoon, as he wandered aimlessly around the yard, Mitch came upon Papa Carl, surprising them both. In the seconds before Papa Carl looked up and forced a smile, Mitch caught sight of him leaning against the back side of the tool shed, head drooped forward, eyes closed, fingers pinching the bridge of his nose, as if by doing so he'd stop some unbearable pain.

After an awkward moment, Mitch said, "I have to go to the bathroom," and took off for the house, ashamed.

Cherry said to no one in particular, "Someone's been sitting on the sofa with a wet bathing suit. Again."

Papa Carl said to no one in particular, "I'm going out. I don't know when I'll be home."

Cherry: "Last I checked, groceries weren't free."

Papa Carl: "I could kill Wade Sinclair."

Cherry: "This house seems smaller by the minute."

Mitch started to daydream about the house next door. The *empty* house next door. It seemed to him to provide a good solution to a mounting problem. He and his mother could move in. Papa Carl and Cherry would have their house back, but they'd still be close. Mitch needed them close, right now. Despite the tension that enveloped all of them like a caul, he loved his grandparents and knew they loved him.

His thoughts about the house may have begun as a whim, but they'd become serious. Firm, possible; a decision. He'd start to make the house his own, little by little. And so he swept the stoop and cleaned the birdbath and sat under the back porch and carved his initials into the front-porch railing, thinking that each thing he did would somehow bring him closer to ownership. If he could believe the impossible truth that his father had left him and his mother, then he could believe that this house was there for the taking. Didn't it make sense that after something horrible happens, something better should follow?

The morning after he carved his initials into the porch railing, Mitch checked the local newspaper to see if there were any nearby houses for sale or rent. He wanted to get an idea of how expensive the house next door might be. He found nothing, so he tracked down his grandmother. She was in the kitchen, chopping vegetables at the table. Her pale, veined hands worked expertly.

"Cherry, what does a house around here cost?" Mitch asked. "To rent or to buy," he added.

Cherry looked up, her paring knife poised in midair. "I don't know, exactly," came the slow reply. "I really don't." Her voice had an edge of testiness to it. She resumed chopping. *Chop, chop, chop.*

Mitch pressed on, "Do you know what's going on with the house next door? The white one. I think it's empty."

"House next door?" Cherry came down hard with the knife, and a piece of celery shot across the room like a bullet. "I don't even know what's going on in *my* house. How would I know about the house next door?" She directed a withering look her grandson's way.

Mitch's throat knotted. "Sorry," he whispered.

Silence.

Cherry bomb, thought Mitch, eyes skimming the floor for the celery piece.

Again: *chop, chop, chop.* Then: stop.

Little disturbances rippled across Cherry's face. "No, *I'm* sorry." She sighed, and her sharp, pinched expression turned soft. "That house has been vacant ever since we retired here," she told him. "I think the owners are from Madison. I've seen a man over there once or twice, checking on things. A yard service cuts the grass, if you want to call it that. More like dirt and weeds. That's about all I know." She paused, then laughed wearily. "My patience is wearing thin, but I shouldn't lose my temper with you. You're only twelve. I tend to forget that." She reached out and touched his hand, a feathery touch. If his eyes had been closed, he might not have felt it.

The sky was ice blue. The air was motionless. The sun hammered down. Mitch took a quick swim, dried off, then spent a good part of the day under the porch of the vacant house, hiding from the world. To get under the porch, he'd slide a broken, latticed panel aside just far enough, so that he could squeeze through. Then he'd pull the panel back into place, crawl over to the foundation, and sit.

His interaction with Cherry bewildered him. How come, he wondered, it's so hard to love all the people I'm supposed to love? He squinted out through the diamond-shaped pattern of the lattice-work. His mind turned fast, from Cherry to his father. He wondered when he'd see his father again. He wondered: Is he thinking of me right now?

Without realizing it, Mitch had brought his finger—the one with the splinter—up to his mouth and was playing it against his teeth. The finger hurt when he thought about it, and when he really concentrated on it, it hurt a lot. The tip was red. He'd decided to keep the splinter. He reasoned that the splinter was part of the house, and so, now, part of the house was embedded in him. And didn't that make it more likely that the house would eventually belong to him and his mother? The splinter would be his good-luck charm. He ran his finger under his T-shirt, lightly touched his heart, and wished.

Suddenly, a squirrel appeared at the panel. It moved its head from side to side in small, jerky increments, then darted off. "Lucky, stupid little thing," Mitch whispered.

"Mitch!"

He heard his mother calling him. He got down on his hands and knees and crawled forward so that his face was against the latticework. He watched her.

"Mitch!" She broke through the row of lilacs that divided the two yards. She looked uncertainly up toward the house, down toward the lake. Appearing defeated, she threw out her arms, then let them drop to her sides. She stood completely still for a moment, turned, and headed back in the direction of Papa Carl and Cherry's.

He didn't want her to know where he was, so he

waited until she was out of sight before he followed her, calling, "Mom! Here I am!"

After lunch, and again after dinner, he headed for his spot under the porch. Both times he brought things with him. After lunch, he brought hand clippers to trim some of the weeds at the edge of the porch, a can of root beer, and an old, stained cushion, from his grandparents' garage, on which to sit. After dinner, he brought duct tape to repair, as best he could, the broken latticework, and another can of root beer. He also brought a photograph he'd taken from one of his grandparents' albums.

In the photograph, Mitch and his parents were standing close together, arms entwined, with Bird Lake in the background. Everyone was smiling. Mitch remembered the day from the previous summer as a twinkling jewel of a day. They'd fished, swum, eaten outside on a blanket. Mitch and his father had played catch with a football, too, every chance they could (Mitch was trying to perfect his spiral), even after the sky had been drained of light and the ball had become ghostly, almost invisible.

Using the duct tape, Mitch fastened the photograph to one of the boards above him, the underside of the porch. He could see the photograph if he wanted to, by leaning back and looking up.

As the sun lowered, a weak puddle of light slanted closer, creeping across the dirt into his realm. Soon everything would be dim and blue and quiet, like a bigger version of the dusky place—his room—under the porch. He didn't mind being here, alone. This particular solitude was becoming familiar to him, and not unpleasant. After a while he grew oddly calm, and just as he had gotten perfectly settled, comfortable on the old cushion, something happened.

It was the slamming of the car doors that he heard first. One-two-three-four. Then a large dog tore past him, down to the lake, and ran back, responding to its name: "Jasper! Jasper, come!"

The air was electric.

"We're really here," he heard a boy say.

"That didn't take very long," said a girl.

"Let's unload the car before we do anything else," said a man.

"We'll go down to the lake together," said a woman.

"Listen to your mother." It was the man again. "I mean it."

Minutes later, footsteps could be heard directly above him. These people, whoever they were, were on the screened porch, separated from him by mere inches. A couple of the boards creaked and sagged with their weight. He felt a clutch of fear. His heart beat faster, faster. He sat, barely moving, pinned to the cushion by what was happening.

"Hurry, hurry," said the boy.

"It'll be okay, Mom," said the girl.

The dog barked and paced across the porch, his nails clicking on the floor like drumbeats.

"I'm ready," said the boy. "Let's go to the lake."

"Just a minute," said the man.

"I can't believe this is ours," said the girl.

Mitch held his breath. His skin was slick with sweat. He felt the girl's voice, her words, throughout his entire body. He had been scared, and now he was indignant, too.

*I can't believe this is ours.*

No, it's not, he thought. It's mine.

## 2 ● SPENCER

Matty's death had been absorbed into the fabric of the Stone family. It was a fact, rarely mentioned, that, in combination with hundreds of other facts, made up the complete picture of who this family was. It was one stitch in a tapestry. That's the way it seemed to Spencer Stone anyway, until the summer that he was ten.

It was on a listless June night, after dinner, that Peter and Emmy, Spencer's parents, brought up the topic of Matty. Spencer's mother seemed particularly serious, guarded. Spencer, his parents, and his seven-year-old sister, Lolly, were on the back porch eating ice cream. Their dog, Jasper, lay at their feet—a lumpy, hairy heap of a rug. The weather had been hot and dry for days. The *tish, tish, tish* of a neighbor's sprinkler blended with the night noises, sounding like a swarm of insects in the near distance. Against the dark vault of the sky, the moon was so bright it seemed close enough to touch.

"How dreadfully lovely," said Lolly in an affected British accent. She stuck out her pinkie dramatically and fluttered her eyelashes as she raised her spoon to her mouth. With a flourish, after each bite, she touched the corners of her mouth with the spoon. Left, right, left, right.

"Weird," whispered Spencer.

"There's something we'd like to talk about," said Spencer's mother, exchanging a meaningful glance with Spencer's father. She straightened in her chair.

Spencer shrugged and looked from one parent to the other, only half curious because the ice cream tasted so good and because his mother's tone led him to believe that she was not going to say anything interesting but rather something about responsibility. A lecture. Spencer couldn't remember if he'd made his bed that morning. He guessed that there were dirty clothes, books, and who-knew-what-else strewn across his bedroom floor as usual. He concentrated fiercely on the ice cream—chocolate, cold, delicious, smooth—trying to stop time, trying to keep his mother from talking.

"Are you listening?" asked his father.

"But of course," said Lolly, still using the accent.

"Yeah," said Spencer. So much for stopping time. He braced himself.

"We're going to be taking a little vacation," said Spencer's mother.

"I know," said Spencer, somewhat relieved but still wondering if the lecture was lurking just around the corner. "To Michigan to see Gran and Poppo."

"No," said Spencer's father. "I mean, yes. Yes, we're going to Michigan. That's in August—same as always—but this is a different trip."

"Disney World!" said Lolly. She'd dropped the

accent. She opened her mouth wide and tapped her spoon lightly against her teeth in excitement. Her teeth were tiny, but they crowded her mouth, and the bigger, serrated, permanent front ones were slightly tilted, like tombstones in an old, untended graveyard.

"Not Disney World," said Spencer's father.

"We're going to Bird Lake," said Spencer's mother.

"What's Bird Lake?" asked Lolly.

Spencer narrowed his eyes and cocked his head. Bird Lake. "I know about Bird Lake," he heard himself say.

"I don't," said Lolly. "*Do* I? What's Bird Lake?"

"It's where Matty died," said Spencer.

"Oh, yeah," said Lolly. "I knew I heard of it."

"Why are we going there?" asked Spencer.

And they told them.

First, they spoke of the history of the place, reminding Spencer and Lolly that the house at Bird Lake had belonged to Emmy's mother and father. When they died, the property had become Emmy's.

Even though he knew this information, Spencer listened intently. Lolly seemed less interested. She quietly collected the empty ice-cream bowls and placed them methodically on the floor in a row by Jasper so that he could lick them clean.

Matty had drowned at Bird Lake when he was four years old. Spencer was two at the time and had no memory of it—the drowning nor Bird Lake. "And I wasn't even born yet," said Lolly. "So, of course, I didn't cry."

Moths, drab and lumbering, had been drawn to the overhead light as if this conversation were important, as if they were listening, too. They batted about and subsided, then batted again.

"We've had the property all these years without using it," said Spencer's mother. "And your father and I decided that it's time either to sell it or to have it be part of our lives again."

"So we're going next week," said Spencer's father. "To check it out. Sort of a trial run."

Spencer nodded. He compressed his lips until they disappeared.

"I loved it there when I was a girl," said Spencer's mother, her voice thickening. "I think you might love it, too."

"Yeah," said Spencer. It was one of those rare moments in which he felt compelled to make some kind of reassuring gesture for his mother's sake: a hand on her shoulder, a tap on her arm, something. The kind of thing a parent would do for a child. He managed a timid smile.

"It's not Disney World," said Lolly, "but I'll go anyway."

"Thank you, Your Highness," said Spencer's mother.

"And no one will have F.M.S. because we'll all be there together," said Lolly. In Spencer's family, F.M.S. stood for "fear of missing something."

"That's right," said Spencer's father. "No F.M.S. for anyone. We'll all be there together."

A house on a lake. Spencer's eyes brightened. He felt a sudden twitch of excitement; it spread over him like a stain.

● ● ●

That night in bed Spencer thought about Matty, and the next day Matty was never far from Spencer's mind. The preoccupation grew, but not in a troublesome way. Throughout the week before they left for Bird Lake, Matty was there, like a shadow, or a song you can't get out of your head.

There were three photographs of Matty in the house: one of him as a baby, one as a toddler, and one from his first day of preschool. They hung among dozens of other photographs, mostly of Spencer and Lolly, on the wall along the staircase. The preschool photograph, more than the other two, provided Spencer with the mental image of his brother: a round-cheeked, sandy-haired boy in a striped shirt with long-lashed eyes, a comical grin, and potato knees. It was odd to think that Matty would be twelve years old if he were alive. No matter how hard he tried, Spencer could not conjure up a mental image of that.

For Spencer, the only other reminder of Matty in the house was a tiny ivory turtle on the mantel. The story was that when Matty was two, he had swallowed it. It sat by a pair of brass candlesticks, unobtrusive as a pebble, barely noticed.

On the morning of the day they were to depart for Bird Lake, Spencer picked up the turtle and held it for a few minutes. It felt smooth and was cool to the touch. He turned it over and over in his hand. When he replaced it, he nudged it across the mantel, through a fine layer of dust, until it was exactly halfway between the candlesticks, the little knob of a head facing straight forward.

By the time the car was packed and the house put in order, the bright sun was starting to sink. For no reason in particular, right before he ran out the front door to leave, Spencer crossed the living room to the fireplace to look at the ivory turtle one last time. The turtle was gone. Someone else was thinking of Matty.

"Will we get there before dark?" Spencer asked his father, speaking loud enough to be heard over the music on the radio.

"Yes, will we get there before dark?" Lolly echoed, but sounding like an old woman with a high, twittering voice.

"Hope so," was the terse reply from the front seat of the car.

"I hope so, too, sonny," Lolly said, looking at Spencer and plucking at his sleeve to get his attention.

Spencer felt heat flood his face. Lolly's voices were annoying him to the point of exasperation. He so wanted to hit his sister, but he kept his emotions in check. He didn't want to upset his parents, especially his mother, by fighting with Lolly. He shook his head in disgust, turned away in frustration, and stared out the window. The clouds were billowy. A passing airplane left a white tail behind it like a vein in the sky. His hands were restless; he drummed his fingers on his thighs.

They'd been on the road for what seemed like a long time to Spencer. First they'd stopped at the frame shop his parents owned to make sure that everything was taken care of before they left on their trip. Next they'd gone to the pharmacy for sunscreen and bug spray. Then, after they'd driven awhile, they'd stopped at a nondescript diner just off the highway by a sea of tall grass tangled with weeds.

"I've eaten here before," Spencer's father had said. "It's pretty good. And Jasper can get out and run around."

They ate outside at a wooden picnic table that was shaded by a large yellow umbrella.

"I'm not very hungry," said Spencer's mother. "I'll take Jasper for some exercise." She left her barely touched sandwich and fries and walked off with the dog along the edge of the bordering field.

"Is Mom okay?" Spencer asked his father when his mother was clearly out of earshot.

"She's a little sad."

"Because of Matty, right?"

Spencer's father nodded.

"But she'll be okay?" said Spencer. He imagined the turtle from the mantel in her pocket.

"I think so. Yes. Yes, of course."

"Are you sad, too?" asked Lolly.

Spencer kicked her under the table.

"Yes," he said, "I am. But I'm happy, too. I'm happy to be taking both of you to Bird Lake." He smiled vaguely and lifted one eyebrow. His voice changed in tone, became lighter, jokey. "And I'm happy to be the father of the two most extraordinary children ever to walk the face of the earth."

"Well, I'm not sad," said Lolly in her British accent. "Not one little bit." She angled her head back and flared the wings of her nostrils.

Spencer shot her a harsh look, unblinking. It went unnoticed.

They finished eating, Spencer's mother and Jasper returned, and everyone piled into the car. In the far back, Jasper circled and circled, then settled down, curling up like a cashew. Right away, Spencer's mother tuned the car radio to a classical station, turning the volume up and up. Normally Spencer would have complained, but he didn't.

On the road again, Spencer felt a certain mysterious

sorrow for his mother. He'd never felt terribly sad about Matty. Sometimes he thought he remembered him, but he wasn't sure. Maybe what he remembered were only stories he'd been told and the photographs he'd seen.

Lolly pierced the cocoon of his thoughts. "I named my voices," she said quietly in her regular voice, as if this were serious business.

"You're a nut," said Spencer.

Lolly elaborated, undeterred. "The old lady one is named Mrs. Mincebottom. The British one is called Gloria Crumpet. And the Southern one is Susanna McCorky." Lolly's green eyes were flecked with amber, and they sparkled as she spoke.

"Really, truly, you are a nut," said Spencer.

"I love nuts," said Lolly as Susanna McCorky.

"We should tie you on top of the car like a Christmas tree," said Spencer. "You could wear my swimming goggles."

"Dear boy," said Lolly as Mrs. Mincebottom, "there wouldn't be room with the kayak and all the other stuff that's already up there."

Accepting defeat, Spencer looked out the window again. Low sunlight gilded everything now. The clouds were like lumbering apricot-colored elephants with huge, round bellies. For just a moment, the car seemed to be made of gold.

They arrived. And there it was. The house at Bird Lake.

Darkness was gathering quickly, so that the details of the house were starting to disappear, to become part of the dusky shadows. But Spencer could see clearly enough to know that he was happy to be here.

It was strange how excited he was. He wanted to hurry to the lake, but his father said to wait. "Wait until your mother's ready," he whispered. Jasper didn't wait—he ran down to the water and came back, then ran around the perimeter of the house playfully, stopping to bow before darting off in the opposite direction.

Spencer forgot about Lolly. And Lolly forgot about her voices, and suddenly appeared to be aware of her mother's mood, and grabbed her hand.

They unloaded the car first, Spencer working eagerly, being helpful. He made a hasty survey of the inside of the house, then he joined his family on the screened back porch. He sensed that his mother wasn't ready yet, but he couldn't contain himself. "Hurry, hurry," he said, looking at his feet.

He felt drawn to the water, so he moved closer to the screen, right up to it. Lightly, he let his nose touch it. "It'll be okay, Mom," he heard his sister say. Turning, he tried to participate in the conversation, tried to speed things up, but soon realized that his parents would proceed at their own pace, and he allowed them that.

Waiting.

Waiting.

Finally they walked to the lake together.

Spencer sniffed. The air smelled of dirt and water and weeds. Dank. The air had an unusual quality to it, as well. Otherworldly. Nothingness and everything mixed. Spencer could *feel* the air. All around him like a thick coat. Or a heavy blanket draped over his shoulders.

Down at the lake, he and Lolly slipped off their shoes. They walked slowly into the cold, black water. Little waves lapped greedily at their ankles and kissed the shore. *Fip, fip, fip.* If Spencer craned his neck a certain way, the moon, which was nearly full, looked as if it were caught in the branches of the big willow tree at the water's edge like a lost ball. Behind him, the lights they'd turned on in the house punctuated the night.

"Stay near," his mother said.

He felt as if he were being watched. By someone or something other than his parents. I don't believe in ghosts, he told himself.

He also felt as if he were still waiting. Everything seemed to be waiting: his mother, the moon, the lake, the house.

For what?

## 3 ● MITCH

Who were these people? Mitch wanted to see them in daylight, really see them, so that he knew what he was up against. Then he could form a plan. He had an idea, but he'd need to think it through carefully. It could either be brilliant or disastrous. He wasn't sure.

The intruders—that's how Mitch thought of the people. The name had come to him the night before as he'd sat under the porch, huddled tight as a fist, terrified that he'd be spotted.

It was the dog that nearly gave him away. While the family was down by the lake, the dog nosed around at the back porch like a bloodhound in a cartoon. His swinging tail and bouncy hindquarters kept knocking against the latticework panel—the only thing protecting Mitch, keeping him from being discovered. Mitch hoped that it was the scent of a passing rabbit, or something like it, that had captured the dog's attention, and not the scent of a boy. Him.

Mitch had wanted to bolt for his grandparents' house, but he knew that the dog would chase him. Barking? Biting? Because his father was allergic to dogs, Mitch had never had one, and so he wasn't a good judge of a dog's temperament.

Mitch waited until all four of them—man, woman, boy, girl—had gone back to the house. The dog, too, of course. As the man passed by the porch, he said, "I wonder if there's something dead under here. Jasper's surely interested." He gave the latticework panel a gentle prod with his foot. At that moment, Mitch clamped down so hard on his bottom lip that it split open.

Only after he'd heard the dog's nails clicking on the floor above him did Mitch emerge from his hideaway and make a run for it. His heart thrashed wildly as he charged across the yard and fumbled through the row of lilacs. A good-size branch lay on the ground in his wake. And only when he was safely in his grandparents' kitchen did he notice that his lip was bleeding and that his legs were unsteady and that his hands were shaking.

Mitch let out a deep sigh. He went to the sink and gulped down three glasses of water. Then, looking at himself in the small oval mirror above the faucet, he dabbed at his lip with a paper towel.

Suddenly, out of nowhere, his mother appeared. "There you are," she said. "It's dark. I didn't know where you were." The rising inflection at the end of her statement made it more a question. She moved in. Closer. "And what happened to your lip?"

He felt his cheeks go hot. "Oh, I fell," he replied, lifting his shoulders high—a gesture that said, "I don't care."

"Let me see."

"It's fine, it's fine." He turned away from her.

She dragged her finger across the countertop. "You need ice."

"I can do it."

Her eyes, glazed by weariness, seemed to refocus, take him in all over again. She said, "You look like you've seen a ghost."

And, just like that, a thought flashed through Mitch's mind. *A ghost.* He pulled back from his fear and anger and sadness long enough for the thought to sink in. He let his mother get ice and a washcloth and examine his lip. He even let her brush his hair out of his eyes without shrugging her off.

Mitch fell asleep that night, thinking about how to haunt the house next door, thinking about how to drive the intruders away.

Now it was morning, early, and he was stationed at the open window in Cherry's well-stocked, well-organized pantry, waiting for the intruders to emerge. The lilacs partially blocked his view, but if he positioned himself just so, he had a fairly clear look at the intruders' front door. And Papa Carl's binoculars didn't hurt.

Mitch lowered the binoculars to give his arms a break. He'd been resting his elbows on the windowsill, frozen in a pose of concentration, and his arms had become tingly.

He stretched. Blinked. Yawned. There had been that brief moment upon waking when he'd forgotten about his circumstances. But the heaviness returned to his chest, and he'd wondered if it—the heaviness—was simply a condition of his life now, life after his father left. He'd wondered if he'd divide his life this way forever: before he left / after he left. Then he'd remembered about trying to haunt the house, and so he had a purpose and his mood improved, became less a contrast to the clear sky, the brilliant morning light.

He'd eaten a quick breakfast—a few handfuls of Cheerios, right from the box, without sitting down. After that, he got the binoculars and crept to the pantry to wait and watch and plot. (All this was managed without being noticed because Mitch's mother and Cherry were engaged in a serious discussion at the dining-room table, and Papa Carl's truck was already gone.)

At his post by the window, Mitch saw the possibilities unspool before him. He thought he'd begin by doing something small—perhaps leaving an object of some sort on the front porch. Nothing threatening. Just something, that, out of context, might seem to hold larger, strange meaning. An empty root-beer can, or a broken plate, or pieces of candy lined up. Then he'd move on from there. He considered sneaking under the screened back porch in the middle of the night and making noises, but that might be too risky. He also considered eavesdropping to gain some personal information, which he could use to write a cryptic note. Then he could tape the note to their door or to one of their windows. He could fill the birdbath with something gross. He could . . .

His mind was an aquarium, and his thoughts were darting around, this way and that, like little fish.

I just can't get caught, he thought.

All at once, the door flew open and the dog shot out into the yard. Mitch gripped the binoculars tightly, readjusted the focus. Jasper. That was the dog's name. Mitch knew this. Maybe he could use this knowledge against the family somehow. One by one, the family filed out the door and down the stoop. Mitch shrank back a bit, reflexively. He didn't want to be noticed, although it was very unlikely that he would be, from such a distance.

He studied them. The dog was fairly big, shaggy, the color of gingerbread. The man and woman just looked like parents. Mitch guessed that the boy was younger than he was, maybe a year or two. And the girl was younger than the boy. She was probably seven or eight years old. Both the boy and the girl had dull brown hair. The girl's was long, pulled back into a ponytail that swung like a pendulum when she chased after the dog. Seeing the dog in daylight, tail wagging madly, bounding in and out of his line of vision, Mitch realized that it had been silly for him to have been afraid last night. The dog seemed perfectly harmless. Briefly, Mitch wondered if the boy was a potential friend, but he pushed the thought aside.

Through the binoculars, Mitch saw the boy sneak up behind the man and jump, swatting the man's baseball cap off his head. The man turned, laughing, and caught the boy in a playful headlock. The boy was laughing, too.

Mitch felt a stab of jealousy. The circular framing of the binoculars made it seem to him that he was watching a movie. The moment was isolated for him— father, son, together—emphasized, made significant like a lesson.

A memory stirred. Mitch recalled doing the exact same thing to his father last soccer season, after the one game his father had come to. Near the end of the game, Mitch had seen him standing on the sideline, his tie loosened, his shirt cuffs rolled up, his Badger cap, red as a cardinal, tipped low over his eyes. From time to time, he'd yell an encouraging comment. He must have left work early, Mitch had thought.

Afterward, on the way to the car, Mitch found the perfect moment to flick off his father's cap. His father stole Mitch's soccer ball. There was lighthearted sparring back and forth. Mitch ended up wearing his father's cap on the drive home. "Don't get it too sweaty, now," his father had said.

The dog barked just then. Jasper. The man's hat was back on his head. After a look at the lake, they all got into the car. Even the dog. They drove away. And the coast was clear for Mitch to do what he needed to do.

He stashed the binoculars in a cupboard, behind some boxes of pasta and rice that appeared to be about a hundred years old, and turned hurriedly to leave the pantry. He bumped into a folding stepstool that was leaning against the wall. The stool fell, hitting a low shelf and knocking a metal canister onto the floor. The lid came off and sugar spilled out.

"Oh, man," Mitch whispered fiercely.

Instinctively, he looked to the door and was grateful that he had closed it. A few long, painful seconds dragged by. No one came.

He quickly replaced the canister. It was a small mess, but still a mess. He felt anger toward Cherry all of a sudden, misguided, but strong. He found a dustpan and a broom and, with sharp, urgent movements, swept up the sugar. He dumped the sugar into a small brown-paper bag grabbed from a stack on one of the shelves. The last thing he wanted was for Cherry to know what had happened, so he took the bag with him.

Within minutes, he was there. On the intruders' front porch.

Think.

What should he do? What would be the best thing to do?

Without knowing why, Mitch emptied the bag onto the porch. The sugar was a miniature mountain of pure white. He crouched over it and tilted his head to one side, as if he were looking at a work of art. Then he flattened the pile with the side of his hand and traced the pattern of a soccer ball into the sugar with his finger. He drew a hexagon surrounded by a ring of pentagons.

Was that correct? He filled the remaining space with random lines. What he ended up with was a bit too oval shaped and lopsided, but he let it be. And it looked more like a geometric design than a soccer ball, but that added to the perplexing nature of it, he reasoned. Hoped.

He was remembering, once again, the one soccer game his father had come to.

A bird called raucously from a nearby tree, and he realized he'd been in a sort of trance.

He took a slow, deep breath. Beneath the design he carefully formed a number twelve, because he was twelve and because it would make the whole thing seem like a code of some sort. Mysterious. A dead bee lay just beyond the circumference of the sugar. With his pinkie, he nudged it next to the twelve. More mysterious. Sugar stuck to his sweaty finger; he licked it off without really tasting it. He crumpled the bag and held it in his fist.

As he rose to leave, two things caught his attention: his initials he'd carved into the railing the other day and a pair of swimming goggles neatly placed on the edge of the stoop. He picked up the goggles and ran toward his grandparents'. There was dew on the weedy grass, and he slipped twice but didn't fall.

When he reached the tangle of lilacs, he stopped. Camouflaged, he couldn't help casting a glance back, then glancing all around. His heart was drumming and his throat had gone dry. The lilacs, the flowers, were long past their prime, brown, like clusters of scorched popcorn. He debated snapping off a handful and adding them to his creation but decided against it. He could use them later.

He wondered what would happen next.

Everything was still, but in a strange way, as if he were looking and feeling through a filter.

He had started something in motion.

Thrilling.

The car didn't come back and didn't come back, and Mitch grew tired of waiting. But he knew that the intruders weren't gone for good: Their neon yellow kayak was lying on its side against the bushes near the birdbath like a giant electric banana, and several windows on both floors of the house had been left open.

Mitch's stomach rumbled, and he realized that he was hungry. He'd been moving furtively about the yard from spot to spot, places where he could see but not be seen. He decided to go inside to check out the refrigerator. He crossed the lawn and was rounding the corner of his grandparents' house when the telephone rang. Its muffled shrillness sounded out of place to him. At first the ringing seemed faraway, even dreamlike, a distant warning, not of his concern, and then he suddenly snapped into a new level of awareness. A deep, icy feeling clutched his stomach, and he was certain, absolutely certain, that it was his father calling. He raced along the garden, took the steps two at a time, and burst into the kitchen, as though he had been reeled in on a line.

Cherry met him just inside the entryway, her arm extended, the phone in her hand. An offering. "It's for you," she said. "The phone's portable, of course," she added. "But stay near the base or the reception gets fuzzy. I'll leave so you can have some privacy."

With lifted eyebrows and wide eyes, Mitch took the phone. He spread his feet slightly and braced himself. After Cherry had left the room, he said, "Hello?" in a stiff, tentative voice.

"Hey, Mitch, it's Dad."

*I knew it.* "Oh, hi."

"Hi." A pause. "I miss you."

*Whose fault is that?* "Yeah. I miss you, too. Do— do you—" He hesitated. "Do you want to talk to Mom?"

"I want to talk to you."

Silence stretched between them.

Mitch's father cleared his throat, "I want to take you out for dinner tonight. We'll go to that good hamburger place you like. Or wherever you want. Your choice. I'll pick you up around five."

"I'll ask Mom."

"I already did. We talked about it last night. She's okay with it."

"She didn't tell me."

"*I* wanted to tell you."

"Oh." *What else did you talk about?* "So is Mom going, too?"

"No, just the two of us. And bring your football. We can toss it around the parking lot." Another pause, "I'll honk for you. I'll wait in the car."

"Now do you want to talk to Mom?" *Please say yes.*

Mitch's father expelled a breath that seemed to have an edge and go on forever. "No," he finally said. His voice had dropped to a loud whisper. "No need to."

Mitch sucked on his swollen lip, replaying his father's modest, measured response to the last question.

"Oh," said his father, "I've got a present for you. A cell phone. I thought you could use it, you know, under the circumstances, because Mom and I . . ."

Mitch listened intently, afraid he'd hear the words "are getting a divorce." But the sentence was left unfinished. Nonetheless, one of those unspoken words formed in Mitch's mind, each letter as big as a house and made of stone: D-I-V-O-R-C-E.

"Anyway . . . you *wanted* a cell phone, right?"

*Not really.* "Mmm-hmm," Mitch murmured with tight lips, his voice rising in a tight, fake sort of way because he was trying to hide his sadness. Then his mouth fell open; he didn't know what to say next.

"Well, bud, I'll see you later." His father's tone was hushed.

"Okay. Bye."

"Bye. I love you, Mitch."

*Really?* "Love you, too." *Come back. To stay.*

Mitch was reluctant to hang up, so one more time he said, "Bye."

"Bye."

That was it.


After the telephone call, Mitch shifted about moodily on the bed in the spare room, feeling sorry for himself. He'd missed the intruders' homecoming. He knew this because his mother had poked her head into the room and said, "I think there's a family staying in the house next door. They're swimming right now. I saw a boy about your age. Maybe the two of you could play together. Did you see him?"

"Yeah, I saw him. And I also saw that he had a mother *and* a father," Mitch had replied, staring at the ceiling with stony eyes. When he'd turned toward the doorway to catch her reaction and perhaps apologize, she'd already left.

The weight of it all threatened to overwhelm him. He buried his face in his pillow, trying to screen out the world, but random thoughts and images swirled through his head. All the things he tried *not* to think about, were, of course, the things he did.

His father: How would their dinner together be? Would the word *divorce* be mentioned? Or, if Mitch did everything right, could it be the first step toward getting their old life restored? What would it take to get his father to spend the night?

His old house: What would happen to *it*? Would all of them move back eventually? Would he and his mother move back before school started in the fall?

The intruders: Had they seen the front porch? How had they reacted?

His splinter: What if it was infected? What if it gave him some dread disease?

The goggles: What should he do with them? He'd shoved them into one of the small zippered compartments in his backpack. He'd never stolen anything before; he vowed to give them back. But it would have to be done in a clever way, a way that would be useful, part of his plan.

Thinking about stealing caused his mind to drift to a boy at his school. Ross Liscum. Ross had been a bother, like Mitch's splinter, since Mitch was in kindergarten and Ross was a first grader. Ross was the kind of kid who cut in line, tripped people in the hallways, threw fists at sack lunches to crush them, cheated on tests, bragged repeatedly about his athletic abilities, and made venomous comments about other classmates' appearances, which made no sense to Mitch because Ross had a slightly deformed ear that looked like a fortune cookie. Just the kind of thing Ross would taunt others about.

Mitch had been Ross's victim on occasion ("It's *Miss* Sinclair!" Ross would say for no apparent reason), but not with the regularity that others suffered, thank goodness. Secretly, Mitch thought of him as Ross Lip Scum, but he'd never dare call him that.

When Mitch complained about Ross to his parents, they'd always given him the "ignore him" lecture and reminded Mitch that Ross's parents were divorced, as if this were reason enough to be a full-fledged jerk. For the moment, this comment shot to the forefront of Mitch's concerns and settled in. It stung him sharply. I've stolen something, he thought, because my parents are getting divorced.

Mitch tried to think about not thinking. But then the word *think* became all he could think about. *Think-think-think-think-think.* Like the rhythmic clicking of the ceiling fan, a tic in his brain. *Think-think-think-think-think.* Until he was apt to explode.

When he was younger and tried to empty his mind of unwanted worries, Mitch would recall roller coasters he'd ridden on, trying to re-create the different courses in complete detail—each turn, each climb, each drop.

This no longer worked, so he tried conjuring up the image of Julie McNight, who was in his homeroom and half of his classes last year. She was popular and pretty and not part of his circle of friends. And she was a very good writer.

For an assignment in English class just weeks before summer vacation, the students had been told to compose an autobiographical sketch. As part of hers, Julie had written: "I have black hair. But it is not as dramatically black and shiny as Mitch Sinclair's hair, which looks like crows' wings sweeping across his forehead and over his ears." (Mitch had memorized this.)

She'd slid a copy of it, highlighted in lime green, onto his desk as she'd brushed past him the day the assignment was due. An attached Post-it note in the margin at the appropriate spot had the sentiment "I LIKE YOUR HAIR. OBVIOUSLY" printed on it in large rounded letters, followed by five exclamation points and a smiley face.

It felt good to remember the incident. He tried to concentrate on Julie—*her* black, shiny hair and lemony smell and the pink spot on her right cheek the size and shape of a little strawberry. He imagined touching the spot—something he could never do in real life.

Mitch still had the copy of the assignment Julie had given him, folded in half, kept safe in his backpack. He went to retrieve it but got sidetracked by the stolen goggles. A worrisome urgency overtook him, and he decided to return the goggles. Right now. He would not become another Ross Lip Scum.

The intruders were still swimming. The sounds of the happy family—laughter, splashing, and calls of "Marco!" and "Polo!"—rose like smoke and were carried off in the breeze. From the distance of the lilacs, shaded by the dusty leaves, Mitch scrutinized the goggles. He wound and twisted the rubber strap of the goggles around the eyepieces and a small rock he'd found at his feet, to form a tight, tangled knot. He gauged its heft by tossing it a few times from hand to hand. Then he broke out of the lilacs just long enough to hurl it toward the house with all his might. As sometimes happens when one least expects it, the thrown object hit a bull's-eye of sorts. The goggles landed in the birdbath, making the placement of them seem deliberate, like a message nailed to a tree, and Mitch felt certain relief.

It didn't last long; he would spend the rest of the day slipping in and out of a gloomy haze, awaiting his father.


The horn blared. Mitch was ready. Unexpectedly, his spirits had taken an upward turn. He was determined to start the night off right with his father. He shouted a quick good-bye to his mother, then walked out the back door and snuck around the house and along the driveway, weaving between the bushes that bordered it. He moved slowly, clinging to the perfectly manicured shrubs. The horn blared again. Again. Mitch heard the car door open. He bent down low, squinted at the ground, and counted to ten. When he craned his neck and looked ahead and saw the back of his father's familiar red Badger cap, his heart expanded, he felt buoyant. Yes! he thought. Ever so quietly, so as to not make the gravel crunch beneath his feet, he crept up on his father from behind.

The single moment that followed was loaded to overflowing.

Mitch yelled, "Hey!" and thrust out his hand to knock off his father's cap, just like the happy intruder son had done earlier. At that precise instant, Mitch's father jerked his head around (perhaps he'd heard the sound of approaching footsteps), and so Mitch ended up striking his father in the nose and sending his sunglasses skittering across the driveway.

Mitch was embarrassed beyond belief, and to make matters worse, he saw that his father was growing a beard and a mustache. He looked so different. Sort of like his father, but sort of not. He looked strange. The father he knew was obscured, the way Cherry's garden wall was obscured by vines. Was he trying to be a new person?

Out of the corner of his eye, Mitch also noticed his mother and Cherry watching from one of the front windows, half hidden by the curtain.

And Mitch just stood there lamely, stock-still, limp shouldered, as his father, a peculiar expression clouding his face, rubbed his nose and said, "What do you think you're *doing*?"

## 4 • SPENCER

The first thing Spencer did when he woke up was to inscribe his name and address on the inside front cover of the book he'd been reading. But instead of his Madison address, he wrote:

23 Lakeshore Drive

Bird Lake, Wisconsin

Already the house was insinuating itself into his heart. After only one night, he envisioned the house belonging to him one day. And not just as a vacation spot. He imagined himself as an adult living on Bird Lake year-round.

On the outside, in the light of day, the house was

nothing special—just a weary, common box. But the inside was different. The inside felt comfortable to Spencer. He liked the rough carpentry, the antlers and maps hanging from the unfinished walls, the screened porch, and the wide-planked floors throughout, with gaps so wide they looked like furrowed fields. He even found the mismatched dishes and silverware comforting. The unkempt, hodgepodge nature of the house suited him well. He thought that he could be messy here and no one would know the difference. He was relaxed.

His mother wasn't, however. She seemed especially quiet and restless. Her smiles were shadows of her usual smiles. Her eyes wandered, off to the side, searching the distance. He could guess what she was thinking. And so he decided not to push the issue of swimming; he'd wait for her to let him know when the time was right. Which meant they didn't go swimming, right away, that first morning, even though that's what Spencer wanted to do more than anything. Instead they went out for breakfast and to buy groceries.

Because he hoped that she would like the house enough to keep it, Spencer tried to talk it up without being annoying or too obvious.

"I slept great last night," he said cheerfully, settling into the car and fastening his seat belt. "I like it here," he added a minute later as the car pulled out onto the road that hugged the lake and led to town. He braided and unbraided his fingers on his lap, acting nonchalant.

His mother turned partway around and smiled a weak smile. "I'm glad."

They passed the neighbors' house. It was toylike and tidy, almost too tidy. To Spencer it looked as if it were the home of a perfect family in a G-rated, schmaltzy movie. On the other side of Spencer's family's house was a stand of white pines—some majestic, some small and spindly. When the wind blew, the branches did a disorderly, comic dance that was somehow graceful at the same time. Spencer could see a few of the trees, towering above the rooftops, out the back window.

"After we have breakfast and get groceries, *then* can we go swimming?" asked Lolly. "Please?" She pursed her lips into a rosebud.

It was the question Spencer had been reluctant to ask.

"Yes," said his father.

"Finally," said Lolly. "I've already got my suit on." She pulled her T-shirt up, revealing a patch of her new bathing suit—orange, lime, and lemon slices in candy colors.

Spencer fought hard to swallow back a comment about Lolly being a fruit. He did notice, and was grateful, that she wasn't doing her voices this morning.

He leaned into the half-opened window, chin on glass. The lake appeared between the trees, then disappeared, then appeared again. Here and there, the sun glinted on the surface of the water. Shards of pure light. It suddenly struck Spencer that simply gazing at a lake could make someone joyful or mournful. It just depended.

They went to the general store both for breakfast

and to get groceries. Breakfast was first. They ate on benches on a deck overlooking the lake so that Jasper could stay with them. Spencer was too excited to be hungry. He played with his food and snuck scraps of pancake and bacon to Jasper.

Afterward they shopped. The general store was old-fashioned and rustic in a way that made Madison—home—seem like a big city. The wooden floors were so warped, the cart tended to veer from side to side, drawn to the rickety shelving as if by magnets. It cheered Spencer to watch his parents stock up on provisions. Judging by all they were buying, he was certain they'd be spending the entire week at Bird Lake. And there were items in the cart that rarely showed up at home: marshmallows, potato chips, and sugary breakfast cereal.

Spencer's mother drove on the way back to the house. "I want you to see some of my favorite places," she said. "There's the public beach. Oh, and look, Wing Rock. And the old bandstand." She slowed the car to a crawl. "I loved to have my lunch there when I was young. I'd pretend it belonged to me. My own little cottage."

"Did you go there alone?" peeped Lolly.

"No, your grandfather would take me. We'd pick up lunch at the general store and then walk over to the bandstand to eat. I'd spread out my beach towel as a makeshift tablecloth." She sighed.

They meandered around the lake, taking the long route home, angling onto the gravel shoulder to let other cars pass. Spencer was glad that his mother was pointing things out. He thought it meant that she was having a good time.

As the car approached the house, Lolly peeled off her clothes, squirming and contorting her body while managing to stay buckled in her seat belt. Before the engine had stopped running, Lolly's T-shirt and shorts were in a loose bundle at her feet. She sprang from the car before everyone else and trotted around it, her bathing suit vivid as a banner at a carnival.

"Wait for me, Lolly," said Spencer's mother. She handed a set of keys to Spencer's father over the hood of the car. "Peter, will you and Spencer take the groceries in? I'll go down to the lake with Lolly."

"You bet," said Spencer's father.

Spencer saw a knowing look flit between his parents. He couldn't believe what was happening. He wanted to go to the lake just as much as Lolly did. Probably more. He could feel his ears turn pink.

"Spencer," called his father, "go unlock the door. I'll start unloading the groceries. Here—" He tossed the keys to Spencer. "It's the gold one. Turn it to the right."

"Jasper!" yelled Lolly. "Come, Jasper! Come swimming with me!" She slapped her thighs—*whap-whap-whap, whap-whap-whap*—and it felt to Spencer as if she were slapping *him*. Or sending him a message in Morse code: Ha, ha, ha. Ha, ha, ha.

Jasper ran to Lolly.

"No!" It was Spencer. "You can't have everything, Lolly," he said scornfully. "Here, Jasper! Treat! Treat!"

As far as Jasper was concerned, *treat* was the

magic word. His head spun around and he doubled back, gamboling to Spencer like a lamb.

Lolly didn't seem to care one whit; she shrugged and skipped away.

"Good boy," said Spencer. "And always remember to stay clear of the freak posing as my sister." He was talking loud enough for his father to hear, and he did so in a sulky voice.

"We'll be swimming in a few minutes, Spence," said his father. "Don't sweat it."

"Whatever," Spencer mumbled, his chin tucked into his neck. He was in such a hurry and he was so angry, he didn't notice it at first. He thudded bitterly onto the little front porch and it suddenly appeared before his eyes.

It.

What was it?

It was some kind of design. Geometric. Oval shaped. And there was a number twelve, too. Right there. On the floor of the stoop. Drawn in what appeared to be sugar. And he was certain that it hadn't been there when they'd left for the general store. One of them—*all* of them—would have seen it.

"Hey, Dad—" Spencer began, but stopped.

It *wasn't* a geometric design; it was a turtle. The back of a turtle. Like Matty's turtle. And the twelve? Spencer suddenly remembered that Matty would be twelve if he were alive.

A shiver went through Spencer and wouldn't go away, as if a ribbon of ice had been tied to his spine.

He'd only seen the turtle for a second or two before Jasper padded all over it, excited, eager to get his treat.

"Sit," Spencer commanded. And Jasper did, but his tail swished, back and forth, ruining what was left of the turtle and the twelve. Then Jasper went wild, licking up the tiny white crystals until there was nothing left on the porch floor except a dead bee.

Gone. Here and gone, just like that.

Spencer's heart pitched. Had he just received some strange message from his dead brother?

"Hey, Spencer," his father said, coming near, his

arms encircling three bags of groceries, "I thought you were in a blazing heat to go swimming. Now you look like a statue."

"Oh, yeah, sorry," he managed to reply, daunted by what had just happened, what he had just seen.

"Are you having trouble with the lock?"

"Yeah. No. I mean, it's fine." He quickly unlocked the door, held it open for his father, then went to lug the remaining groceries from the car to the house.

Shortly afterward, Spencer was swimming—they all were, even his mother—but some of the anticipated pleasure had been drained from the experience. Repeatedly his thoughts returned to Matty and the sign, or whatever it was, that had appeared on the porch.

There were moments when the joy of slicing through the water or playing Marco Polo or cheering for Jasper as he dog-paddled after a thrown stick fully absorbed Spencer's attention, but invariably he'd pause and lift his head, eyes darting about, perceiving a voltage in the air. Matty? And hadn't he thought that he was being watched last night when they were down at the lake? Had that been Matty as well? Spencer felt more aware than usual, as if something of a spell were upon him and he'd acquired another sense.

Both Spencer and Lolly were good swimmers. Learning to swim—to swim *well*—was something their parents insisted on. Spencer was stronger than Lolly, and faster, but Lolly was not far behind and loved to race her brother. Spencer dreaded the day that she could beat him. He hoped beyond hope that it would never arrive.

After one too many games of Marco Polo, Spencer's parents retreated to the tiny, sandy patch of shoreline partially framed by tall weeds and sat side by side, hand in hand.

"They look like giant children in a sandbox," Lolly observed. She laughed, a high-pitched titter, obviously pleased with her remark. She was using a new voice. To Spencer, it sounded chirpy and mechanical. "Do you know who I am?" she asked.

"Not really."

"I'm Birdy Lake. Get it?"

"Duh. Not funny." Spencer was still holding a grudge about her running off to the lake before him, so he couldn't help but add, "Can't you just be a normal person and talk in a normal voice? I know that normal for you is slightly *ab*normal to most people, but you understand what I mean."

Lolly licked her lips and tightened them into a line. They were standing several feet apart, waist-deep in the lake. Lolly raised her hands and dabbled with her fingers in the water between her and Spencer. A few sparkling droplets clung to her eyelashes, and fleetingly, Spencer saw them as tears and wondered if she were crying.

"I'll stop talking like this if you'll race me," Lolly said.

"Promise?"

"Promise. I, Birdy Lake, solemnly promise to stop talking like myself—"

He cut her off. "Okay, okay. I'll race you, but first I need to get my goggles. I'll be right back."

Spencer never raced Lolly without his goggles. They were the closest thing to a good-luck charm he'd ever had. He'd not lost to Lolly yet and didn't want to start now.

He dried off quickly and headed for the house.

"Where are you going ?" asked his mother.

He stopped and turned. "To get my goggles."

"I saw them in the grass this morning," she told him, "when I took Jasper out. They were by the car. I put them on the front porch before we went to town. Near the edge by the top step."

Spencer cocked his head. "Huh, that's funny," he said, feeling strange again, uncertain, because he knew there was nothing on the porch. "I could swear I put them in the side pouch of my blue bag at home when I packed."

"They must have fallen out when we carried our things in last night."

He ran. He saw that the porch was clear; nonetheless, he stepped onto it tentatively. He searched carefully through the patchy, untrodden grass growing beside the steps, parting it over and over with his hands, reasoning that Jasper could have knocked the goggles off the porch with his tail. Nothing.

In the house, he examined his duffel bag and backpack, checked under the bed and through the drawers of the dresser that had been designated his. Again, nothing. He even rifled through Lolly's things with no success.

What's going on? he wondered.

On his way back down to the lake, Spencer's eyes scanned all about: high, low, forward, backward. He crisscrossed the yard. The stiff grass and weeds were sharp under his bare feet. "Ouch," he said to himself. "Ouch, ouch, ouch."

He came upon the birdbath and froze. He thought he recognized his goggles lying in the shallow pool of water, but they'd been twisted somehow, made compact. After a quick intake of air, his breathing became short and shallow. He picked up the small bundle as if it were poison. Then he shook off the water and untangled his goggles. At the center was a stone.

He felt dizzy. The goggles were surely his, and they seemed fine, except that one of the eyepieces had a few new spidery scratches on it. Handling the stone was not something he wanted to do, but he was inclined to keep track of it, so he plopped it back into the birdbath. There was nothing special about it—it was just an ordinary gray stone.

Passing clouds slipped in front of the sun and one big shadow engulfed him suddenly, like a net dropping over him from above. Seconds later, the shadow lifted.

"Spencer! Hurry up!" Lolly's voice rang out.

"Coming, coming," he muttered, confused by all of it. He longed to be near his family. With his goggles firmly on his head, eyepieces pulled up onto his bangs, he joined them.

"I see you found the goggles," his mother said, smiling.

"Yeah," he replied, edging toward the lake, straight to Lolly, so that he wouldn't have to lie to his mother. "Thank you."

"I'm waiting," yelled Lolly.

When he was close enough to talk quietly, he asked, "Did you take my goggles from the front porch?"

"No," said Lolly. "They're on your head."

"I know that. But that doesn't mean you didn't take them from the porch. Did you? Did you take them and hide them?"

Lolly's face twisted into a look of pure confusion.

"Answer the question. Did you take my goggles?"

"No. Why would I take your stupid goggles? I know you won't race without them, and I want to race you." She paused. "Jeez."

Spencer believed her, truly believed her. "Okay. Sorry."

"Let's race," said Lolly.

They agreed on a starting point and a finish line, a distance deemed fair by both.

As Spencer lowered his goggles over his eyes and secured them, he considered confiding in Lolly. "Do you feel like something is about to happen?" he asked in a small, private voice.

"Yeah, we're going to have a race."

"No, I mean . . . Forget it." But it did feel that way to him—that something was about to happen. The air and the water seemed to be teeming with mystery.

Spencer shook out his arms and rotated his shoulders in preparation for the race. He squinted in resistance to the piercing sunlight on the surface of the water, and caught his bottom lip between his teeth in concentration. That was when an urgent and eerie thought occurred to him: Matty's presence is in the lake. It's all around me. It's touching me. The thought was taking hold when Spencer felt something against his leg. "Ahh—" he cried, terrified to the bone.

Lolly shrieked with laughter. "It's Jasper! He really scared you!"

An understatement. Spencer's heart was hammering inside his chest with the force of a thunderstorm. Can your heart suddenly be twelve sizes too big for your body? Jasper brushing against Spencer's leg had felt like a brush with death itself.

Jasper had a stick in his mouth. Lolly pried it

away from him and threw it toward the shore. "Let's try again," she said to Spencer. "On your mark—"

"I don't want to race," Spencer told her. He flipped off his goggles and followed Jasper. His teeth were chattering.

"What's wrong?" Lolly asked.

"Nothing," was the spoken answer. The real answer: everything.

Spencer sat by his parents, lakeside, and stayed near both or one of them the rest of the day. Was he seeking protection? Safety?

He reminded himself that the incident in the lake was simply Jasper pawing his leg. There was nothing mysterious about that. And he reasoned that there must be logical explanations for the goggles in the birdbath and the turtle drawn in sugar on the porch. Everything has a logical explanation, he repeated in his head. Although for the life of him, he hadn't a clue as to what the explanations could possibly be.

He also reminded himself that nothing out of the

ordinary had happened inside the house. And despite the strangeness of the two incidents, he still loved the house, still wanted to keep it. And so he decided not to tell his parents anything. Who knew how they'd react? And telling Lolly was out of the question— she'd blabber for sure.

Spencer also tried to comfort himself with the thought that even if there were such things as ghosts (impossible), this ghost would be okay because it would be Matty. If Matty were a ghost, he'd undoubtedly be benevolent. After all, he was only four years old when he died.

"Do you think there are ghosts?" Spencer asked his father. Lunch was finished, and the two of them were washing the dishes in the cramped kitchen.

"Absolutely not." And then, as if his father sensed the nature of the concern behind the question, he placed his hands on Spencer's shoulders, and gently squeezed them, saying, "Why do you ask?"

"No special reason."

●　　●　　●

The day passed slowly. As the sunlight weakened, Spencer's brooding increased. In the privacy of his imagination, the idea that Matty was somehow present, sending signs, seemed plausible and grew as the afternoon wore on.

Almost anything could be construed as a sign: The three-sided winged maple seedling that fell at his feet in the yard. The drab little bird that seemed to be following him, twittering, twittering. The mildew that looked like a face on one of the leaves of the wild rosebush near the road. The rust stain in the kitchen sink that he noticed late in the afternoon but hadn't seen when he'd done the lunch dishes earlier.

Were there shapes to be found and deciphered within the dark rectangles of the windows as seen from outside?

Were the fireflies—pinpricks of topaz that flared and vanished in rhythmic patterns—trying to communicate with him?

Before bed, Spencer and his mother admired the moon. His mother said, "A full moon on our first full day here—I take that as a good sign."

"Do you believe in things like that?" Spencer asked. "Signs?"

She sighed and tilted her head upward, rubbing her neck. "Not really. Well, sort of." She smiled. "Actually, yes, tonight I do."

That was not the response he wanted to hear.

## 5 ● MITCH

Mitch dreamed that he was at a restaurant with his parents. Pastel-colored balloons and crepe-paper streamers dripped from the ceiling, the streamers wimpling in the air above him, grazing his hair. The noise level was high. Music, laughter, the clatter of dishes, and the rise and fall of multiple conversations mixed together and had a collective pulse. The light in the room was so bright that everything and everyone looked washed out, bleached. Mitch and his parents were eating all of Mitch's favorite foods: onion rings, grilled-cheese sandwiches, pizza, sweet potatoes with marshmallows, glazed doughnuts. They sipped chocolate shakes through straws. The walls spun gently, and Mitch swiveled his head from shoulder to shoulder, liking the sensation and smiling. He was truly happy. Everyone was. He angled his head back, opened his mouth, and crowed like a bird.

Mitch woke up hearing himself making an odd sound: "Ahh . . ." His pillow was damp with drool. It was a good dream, and yet it had the effect of a bad one.

He sat up and blinked. Details of the dream were fading quickly, edged out by the here and now, but the feeling of being with both of his parents lingered.

He could fight off the tears only so long. Alone, in bed, he gave in and cried quietly into his pillow. Any hope he'd had about his parents getting back together had been extinguished earlier that night at dinner with his father.

They'd been at Smiley's Hamburger House on the outskirts of Bird Lake. Mitch had waited until he'd eaten most of his onion rings before he'd pressed his father. "Are you and Mom getting divorced?" he'd asked, point-blank, surprised by the harshness of his tone.

His father cleared his throat, "Well, we should be with Mom when we get down to specifics. But we've got a lot to figure out before we do that. I thought tonight we could just talk about other things. For starters, what happened to your lip?"

Mitch was feeling bold, more bold than he'd ever felt with his father. "Please, answer the question."

"Well . . . " Mitch's father tossed his right hand up as if he were throwing something at the ceiling. Then he made the same gesture with his left hand.

Mitch's eyes bored right into his father's. But he could only maintain the intensity for a few seconds before a twinge of guilt caused him to stop.

His father struggled, "All right, yes—what do you want? Yes, we're probably—we are getting divorced."

The boldness was gone. Mitch was left with a tightening throat, the beginnings of tears. "Probably?" came Mitch's quiet question.

"Not probably. Not probably."

Where they were, what they were eating, the time of day—all of it became insignificant. Mitch was surrounded by nothingness.

"This isn't about you, bud. What I mean is— none of this is your fault. Listen to me—we both love you and always will. That's the bottom line."

Mitch was silent. He let his eyes drop but sensed his father's steady gaze upon him. Mitch's inner voice spoke: Do not cry. He willed himself into a human fist.

"We'll make the best of it," his father stated unconvincingly.

They were sitting in a booth. Mitch's legs were sticking to the burnt orange upholstery. So was the back of his shirt. When he leaned into the table, his shirt resisted. He pulled forward and leaned back and pulled forward a little more. As his shirt peeled away from the back of the booth, it made a whispery sound that he felt as much as he heard: *schrishhh*.

"Hey, I've got that cell phone for you."

The cell phone was presented. It lay on the

tabletop, midway between them, in a swath of late sunlight, thick and golden. Mitch listened half-heartedly to his father's instructions for using it.

When they left the restaurant, Mitch jammed the cell phone into his pocket, but when he got into the car, he slipped it unnoticed under the seat. He'd leave it there.

On the drive back to Papa Carl and Cherry's, Mitch's father spoke the only words: "Some moon, huh?" And it was. It rose out of the gathering dark-ness, above the gray blur of trees. The moon was significant—pearly, tinged with orange—and seemed to mark the day. A big period, saying: It's official. It's over. Everything's over. It reminded Mitch of the moon on the poster hanging in his pediatrician's office, which he'd always assumed was fake, a doc-tored photograph. He stared vacantly at the unlucky moon and thought, I will always hate full moons.

In the morning, Mitch went to the library with his grandparents. His mother had already left for

Madison to see a lawyer and to have lunch with a friend.

She'd appeared suddenly at the side of his bed to say good-bye. He'd feigned sleepiness, rolling over toward the wall and mumbling into the tangle of blankets. "I'm sorry about last night," she'd told him.

A few minutes later, Papa Carl had shown up in the doorway. "After you get something to eat," he'd said, "come with me."

"All right," Mitch had replied in a soft, almost apologetic voice. He'd thought that his grandfather had meant fishing, and was surprised, at breakfast, to learn that Papa Carl was going to the library to look at woodworking magazines.

"I'm going, too," Cherry had said. "Let's get you some books."

Even if it hadn't been intentional, Mitch felt as though Papa Carl had tricked him, let him down like everyone else. He felt trapped inside the warm, sunny car.

Papa Carl stole glances at Mitch by turning his

head or catching Mitch's eyes in the rearview mirror. Papa Carl had a square jaw and long earlobes. His skin was darkly tanned and was laced with so many wrinkles it looked as if a child had scribbled all over him with a pencil.

"A lot of people get divorced now," he said, his head facing forward again. "Not like when I was a boy."

"There's no disgrace for the child involved," Cherry added curtly. She sat, rigid. Her bony shoulders and short, gray, frizzed-up hair were unmoving, giving the impression that she was balancing an invisible tray of glassware on her head.

Mitch knew that they were speaking loudly for his benefit but couldn't muster a response other than a cluck of his tongue.

The library was a small, rose-colored brick building. It had a certain quality about it—properness—that it shared with Papa Carl and Cherry's house.

"If you need assistance, the librarian is very good," Cherry told Mitch. She touched his elbow as they entered through the heavy wooden doors.

Mitch wandered about the nearly empty air-conditioned rooms as quietly as possible, so as not to draw attention to himself. Periodically he could hear Cherry's footsteps on the highly polished floors. He wanted to see if there were any books about divorce but was too embarrassed to ask the librarian for help, and would have been too embarrassed to check them out anyway.

At one point, he rounded the corner of a tall set of shelves and nearly collided with the librarian. "Are you finding everything you need?" she asked. Her face was open and kind, her cheeks ruddy.

Mitch nodded.

Eventually he sat by himself at a lone table in a corner and leafed through back issues of *Sports Illustrated* and *Rolling Stone,* sometimes paying attention, sometimes thinking of other things.

He knew several kids whose parents were divorced, and that didn't bother him one bit. But those parents weren't *his* parents. He knew that all "divorced kids" (his new term) were not like Ross Liscum. He even knew a divorced kid whose parents each had a separate apartment. The kid lived in his own house, and the parents took turns staying with him.

This had sounded interesting, sort of cool, when he'd first heard of it at school, but put in the context of his own life, it seemed off, even scary, as if the kid were the adult and the adults were the kids.

Growing impatient, he wandered some more, ending up, by chance, at a section of books about dogs. He tried to identify what breed Jasper, the intruders' dog, was. He decided that Jasper must be a mutt, because he couldn't find a photograph or illustration that offered more than a weak resemblance to him.

Mitch abandoned the dog books and stepped noiselessly to the center of the library, where an enormous dictionary lay open on a darkly stained wooden reading stand like two tablets of stone. He fumbled through the thin pages, scanning the entries. He'd intended to look up the words *mongrel* and *mutt* to see if the definitions were the same, when, for some reason, his eyes settled on the word *morass*.

Morass: "something that traps or impedes; a state of confusion or entanglement; any difficult or perplexing situation."

It describes where I am, he thought. I'm in a morass.

"Mr. Mitch?" There was a tap on his shoulder. "Time to go," Papa Carl said in a raspy whisper.

"You can use my card to check out," said Cherry, craning her neck as though she were trying to see what he'd been looking up in the dictionary. "Where are your books?"

"I don't have any," Mitch murmured.

In the parking lot, Cherry said, "At the library for over an hour and not one book. Well, I tried."

"Leave it alone," muttered Papa Carl.

The intruders carried the yellow kayak to the lake, then dragged a canoe down to the same spot. The boy and girl led the dog to the maple tree between the house and the water and lavished him with pats and kisses before latching him to the broad trunk. "Bye, Jasper!" they called. The dog barked a few times, then settled, making himself into a tawny mound that looked like a pile of dead leaves.

It was late morning. Mitch was back at Bird Lake after the trip to the library. He was lying on his stomach, his chin resting in his cupped hands. He stayed low to the ground, inching along beside the lilacs every so often.

Morass. He played with the word in his head until it sounded absurd. He whispered it.

He convinced himself that the intruder son had no firsthand knowledge of what it felt like to be caught up in a morass. And with a jolt of painful awareness came the thought: I will never again have a life like his.

Morass.

As he watched the intruders that morning, Mitch came to the conclusion that his trying to scare them away had been a stupid idea and had had no effect on them anyway. Their behavior—joking around, playing together—was proof enough for him. And something shifted inside him. He no longer wanted the house. He now saw it as shabby and sorry looking. Who needs it?

He realized that he hadn't been swimming since the intruders had arrived. This made him angry.

Morass. Me. Mitch. Mad. Mutt.

M-M-M-M-M.

He waited long after the intruders had paddled out of sight, disappearing behind a clump of brush that jutted out into the lake, before he crawled onto their property. He felt detached, as if he were watching it all from a distance, even as he edged closer.

"Hey, dog," he said softly. "Hey, Jasper."

Jasper's tail wagged in greeting. His eyes were large marbles of the deepest brown with wide black centers; his nose was speckled with pink.

A sudden curiosity inhabited Mitch. It came unbidden and was irresistible.

A temptation.

The action required no thought of which he was aware. No plan. His brain was acting on impulse. Brain to fingers: Do this now.

Mitch extended his hand and unhooked the long lead from around the tree. *Click.* The simplest of movements. Done in a flash.

In that flash, Jasper bounded away, the lead trailing behind him like a thick red snake. Gone.

In that flash, Mitch was filled with overpowering regret.

The morass had increased tenfold.

## 6 ● SPENCER

When he was younger, Spencer had believed that his parents could hear all his thoughts. He no longer believed this, but he still wondered about it. He wondered because sometimes his parents seemed to have radar, seemed to know exactly what he was thinking. And then they'd ask probing questions.

On this particular morning, his thoughts were conflicting and would have been confusing to anyone who was privy to them. On one hand, the odd things that had happened nagged at him and made him wary. On the other hand, the night and the morning had been free of any strangeness, and as he drifted and paddled on the lake, he felt he belonged here, that he was bound to this place. He wore a loose smile to prove it.

He thought that if nothing else out of the ordinary happened, the nagging would become familiar, common as a hangnail, and eventually go away. This was his hope. He also hoped that his mother would ask no probing questions.

Spencer and his mother were in an old, dented aluminum canoe. Spencer's father and Lolly were in the kayak they'd brought from home. And Jasper—he'd refused to get into the wobbly canoe, even when bribed with treats, so they'd left him in the yard, tethered to the maple tree.

The canoe had been stored on the side of the house, beneath the white pines, along with sections of a rotting wooden pier and haphazardly stacked cinder blocks. Fallen needles from the trees covered everything like a patchy winter coat. They'd had to search for paddles. Lolly had found them in a corner in the basement among a cobwebbed jumble of garden tools.

The canoe and the kayak had started out together, but now, nearly an hour into the family's excursion, the two boats were far enough apart that Spencer saw the kayak as a yellow slash on the water, nothing more.

"If you were a tree, what kind would you be?" his mother asked, out of the blue. It was a game they used to play, years ago.

Spencer laughed. "We haven't done this in a long time," he said. It embarrassed him slightly; it seemed babyish. "Um. An oak?" he said, shrugging. "An oak," he repeated firmly. He was thinking of the enormous oak tree in the McDermotts' yard back in Madison. The McDermotts lived next door to the Stones. The oak was good for climbing because of its massive low boughs, and to Spencer, it resembled an elaborate pirate galleon with many gnarled masts reaching up and out. "What about you?" he asked.

"I would be a magnolia tree," she said. "Like the one at home."

He twisted and looked over his shoulder at her in

the stern, and nodded. He was remembering how Lolly used to be convinced that the magnolia tree was female, the McDermotts' oak was male, and that they were married because their branches touched over the fence that separated the yards. The marriage of the trees, she'd said, made the two families related. This misconception of hers had, over time, become part of the Stone family lore.

"Your turn," she said.

"If you were a . . . ," he began slowly. "If you were an animal, what would you be?"

"A turtle," she replied.

Hearing the word *turtle* made him blush. He looked down at the paddle in his hands. He wished he'd said food instead of animal. Or color. Or piece of clothing. Or anything else. He was glad that she was seated behind him and couldn't see his eyes, or his cheeks, which surely were red. Did she know something? Was she trying to ask something indirectly by saying turtle?

Of course he thought of the turtle that had

appeared on the front porch. The sign. He also thought of the small ivory turtle that was missing from the mantel at home. He wondered if his mother had taken it from its usual place. Was it tucked into her pocket this very minute? Was it in her purse? Her wallet?

Or had his father taken it? Or someone—or something—else? He tried to banish these thoughts.

"I'd be a bird," he said, without waiting to be asked for his response. "So I could fly."

Neither tried to continue the game. They were silent for a long time after this. They both seemed to have retreated to private places in their minds. Sitting, as they were in the canoe, made this easier. They weren't face-to-face. There were no probing questions.

Spencer's mother steered them into a little cove. A secret, sheltered inlet. The sun broke through the leaves, dappling Spencer's arms and legs and dotting the water with coins of light.

There seemed to be no noises at all until you really listened, and then, it was as if the world were made of sound. Quick, rushed sounds—the equivalent of scribbling on a notepad. Slow, drowsy ones. The sounds of birds. Of insects. Unseen rustlings from the treetops and from the shadows beyond the shoreline. The lake was a container of sounds, the best one being the musical sound as he pushed the paddle through the water and lifted it out.

"The water is so limpid here," his mother said.

"What's that mean?"

"Transparent. You can see through to the bottom."

"Hmm." He peered over the edge of the canoe. The cluster of rocks below looked like a village as glimpsed from an airplane. The water lapped against the side of the canoe. Spencer gently swayed back and forth. Testing.

"Did you hear that?" his mother asked.

Spencer lifted his head and listened. Did she mean a bird? And then he heard it: a shrill, cheerful cry coming from some distance. Lolly. "Disturbing nature," he said as a joke.

Their idling was over. They started out toward the kayak.

"We'll race you!" Lolly shrieked gleefully when they were within earshot.

"Are you ready to head back?" Spencer's father called. "We're hungry."

"I'm ready," said Spencer's mother.

"But we're not racing," said Spencer.

With the steady wind behind them, they traveled across the lake quickly. From where they were, the cottages ringing the shore looked flimsy, as if they were constructed of balsa wood or cardboard and would blow away if the wind gusted. Spencer didn't want to race, officially, but he did want to beat the kayak back to the house. His strokes were fast and fierce. The muscles in his arms burned. Soon the little house emerged from the background to welcome them. And Spencer and his mother were leading the way.

He was the first one to sense that something was wrong. "Hurry, Mom," he pleaded, "I can't see Jasper." He yelled, "Jasper! Jasper!"

No barking.

No eager dog straining at its leash.

He pumped his tired arms the last bit, exerting all his strength. As the front of the canoe scraped against the pebbles on the narrow beach, he jumped out onto the ground and ran to the maple tree.

"He's gone!" Spencer shouted to his family. His thoughts came, frantic but clear. No concerns about ghosts or spirits entered his consciousness this time. There was no mystery. He knew that Lolly was the one who had hooked Jasper to the tree. He knew that it was all Lolly's fault.

"Mom! Dad! Hurry!"

A couple of minutes later, the four of them stood together in the dark pool of shade by the tree. Spencer couldn't contain himself. He shoved Lolly, accusing her. "Look what you did."

"Spencer, stop," his father said. His voice was firm, and so was his grip on Spencer's shoulders. "What's going on? What are you talking about?"

"Dad, Dad," he said, nearly breathless, "she hooked Jasper to the tree. And he didn't break the leash or chew it. The whole thing's gone. It's obvious what happened. Some people can't even work a simple hook or latch, or whatever you call it." He glared at Lolly. "She didn't do it properly."

Spencer's father had discovered the extra-long leash in the basement while they were looking for paddles. He'd remembered it when Jasper wouldn't go into the canoe. It had seemed sturdy enough. The hook was rusty, but it had seemed sturdy, too. And, unlike the leash they'd brought from home, it was long enough to encircle the tree, which Spencer's father thought was the safest place for Jasper—outside, but far from the water.

The puzzled expression on Lolly's face shifted; something registered, her mouth twitched.

"Shh, shh. Let's just calm down and look around here first," Spencer's mother said. She spoke carefully and plainly. "He's got tags. I'm sure we'll find him. It's no one's fault."

"If we *can't* find Jasper, I'll—" Spencer's words, all snap and sting, ended abruptly.

"Spencer," said his father. A warning.

Spencer snuffled into his arm and swallowed hard.

"I *know* I hooked it," said Lolly. "I *think* I hooked it. It was sort of hard to do, I think. I don't know," she floundered. "I guess it *is* my fault. I'm sorry," she said to no one really, but into the air, her voice more yelping than anything else. She clamped her lips together until she seemed about to explode. Her hands were lumps she lifted to her face, which was already turning blotchy. And then she burst into tears.

While his parents consoled Lolly, Spencer went on at a frantic pace, angry, and with an air of authority. "He could get strangled with that long leash. Or he could drown or get hit by a car or be stolen by some family because he's so friendly."

"Or maybe," Lolly added thoughtfully between sobs, keeping her head down. "Maybe he'll try. To go all the way. Back home. Like the dogs and cat. In that movie we saw."

Spencer spluttered at his sister—a garbled, mean sound. He seemed to be pinning all his uncertainty onto this one thing he perceived as true. It blotted everything else out.

They hollered Jasper's name, whistled for him, circled the house, investigated the lakeshore, looking left and right and left. The little beach was a kaleidoscopic tangle of footprints and pawprints and offered no real help. Then, while they figured out what to do next, they stared at the base of the maple tree as if it would reveal something, some hidden clue.

"Emmy," said Spencer's father, "why don't you and Lolly stay here. Spencer and I will drive around. See what happens."

She nodded. "He'll come back. I know he will."

In desperation, Spencer screamed Jasper's name at the top of his lungs once more.

"Everyone okay?" An old man had passed through the screen of lilacs and was crossing the yard. "Someone lost?"

He walked with a slightly lopsided stride, but quickly. His skin—badly pocked and deeply wrinkled—was the color of wheat bread. He was thin, not too tall.

Spencer peered behind him, expecting Jasper to be in tow. The man was alone.

Introductions were made and explanations were given. The man lived next door, through the lilacs, in the neat and orderly mint green house. His name was Carl. Mr. Burden.

"My grandson, Mitch, is staying with us," said Mr. Burden. "He's around here somewhere. Maybe he could help look for your dog."

Spencer heard something or someone else approaching from the driveway.

"It's my grandson," said Mr. Burden.

"It's my dog!" said Spencer.

The world had been out of order, and now, for the moment, it was right again.

## 7 ● MITCH

He took his grandfather's rarely used bicycle from the garage—with its nearly flat tires and loose, squeaky seat—and rode off without a real plan. He pedaled hard and fast in the direction that Jasper had gone. He yelled Jasper's name a few times but became too self-conscious and decided to search silently.

He wished that he could simply ride and ride and ride and not talk to another person or need anything or anyone again. Ever. Ride and ride and ride until despair had lost its hold.

Not long into his search, he heard a dog barking. He followed the sound, swerving sharply onto a narrow, winding dirt road that led to the lake. His front tire caught in a rut and he fell, scraping his leg on a rock and getting dirt in his mouth. But he lost little time, rising quickly and running down the road, gripping the handlebars with a vengeance, pulling the bicycle along with him as if he and the bike were one.

In a clearing, he saw a girl perched atop an overturned rowboat. A dog was sitting tall beside her.

Jasper! he thought. He threw down the bicycle and approached the girl warily.

"He's mine," said Mitch, tipping his head at the dog. It surprised him how easily the lie had slid off his tongue.

"Prove it," said the girl.

A panicky feeling melted his knees, "Jasper. Come, Jasper," he said, bending slightly and slapping his thighs the way he remembered the intruder son doing.

Mitch's gentle command brought the dog from the girl to him in a flash. He coiled the long leash and held it so tightly that his fingernails dug into his palm.

He would not let go. "Stay?" he whispered tentatively.

The girl jumped off the rowboat. She frowned at Mitch, then placed her hands on her hips and shot him an exaggerated, pouty expression. "Okay," she said, walking toward him. "You win. He's obviously yours."

"Sorry." He noticed that her eyes were shiny with tears.

"I even thought of throwing his tags into the lake," she confessed. "Never to be seen again."

Mitch hadn't read Jasper's tags. If the girl had tested him on Jasper's address, he would have failed. He would have had to come up with a story of some sort quickly.

"Can I pet him one more time?" asked the girl.

"Yeah. Sure."

She came forward and lowered her head to the height of Jasper's and let him cover her face with licks. She scratched him behind his ears. "I would have changed his name," she told Mitch. "I would have called him Kernel. With a K, as in popcorn. Not

Colonel with a C, as in the army or navy or whatever. Cute, don't you think?"

Mitch shrugged.

"My parents won't let me have a dog, and it's all I want. You are so lucky."

If you only knew, thought Mitch. "I've got to go," he said. He turned to leave.

"You are so lucky," she repeated loudly as he walked away.

Her words were so ironic they stung, like stones hurled at his back.

It took some getting used to—riding a bike and holding on to a dog at the same time—but Mitch found a rhythm and Jasper loped along easily. If he slowed down, all Mitch needed to do was to make a clicking sound and say, "Come on, Jasper," and Jasper picked up speed.

Mitch had wanted to get away from the girl as fast as he could, but he'd taken a moment to check Jasper's tags before he'd mounted the bike. The intruders lived in Madison. On a street Mitch didn't know.

He hoped that the intruders were still far out on the lake and that he could put Jasper back where he'd found him. No questions asked. What he'd do if this weren't the case, he could barely consider. Please, please, please, don't be home, he mouthed silently.

Other concerns, scant in comparison, but still concerns: Jasper was wet, had burrs and shredded leaves stuck all over him, and smelled funny, as if he'd gotten into something nasty like a dead fish or someone's garbage.

What would the intruders think? Each problem solved just led to another unsolved one, thought Mitch.

As he neared his grandparents' and the intruders' houses, he felt something—flickers of fear. But something else, too—one tiny glimmer of hope, hope that everything would turn out all right.

Suddenly Jasper charged forward with a burst of energy. Mitch's arm jerked; he was pulled like a rag doll. He thought that a stray cat or a squirrel must be ahead, hidden by bushes or behind a tree or lying low in the ditch at the side of the road. "Whoa, Jasper. Take it easy," he said.

And then Mitch heard whistling. And one mournful "Jasper!" followed by quiet.

Mitch didn't know what to do. Everything was happening too fast. Turning around or taking a break to think it all through was not an option, seeing as Jasper was not to be stopped. Unhooking Jasper or letting go of the leash didn't seem right. Mitch was guilty enough already. Like a twig caught in a river current, Mitch felt he was being carried along, with no control whatsoever over where he was going, with no idea exactly to what he was being taken.

The dog led the boy. On a short, clear, speedy path to some unknown outcome. Up one last stretch of road to the intruders' house, and then down their driveway into their yard, right to the intruders, standing in a tight knot with Papa Carl.

The sight of his grandfather was disorienting

to Mitch. His heart rose up, then seized. What was going on?

Now he let go of the leash.

What he would remember most about that moment was a feeling of pure, intense relief. What he wouldn't remember was who spoke first or what he or she said.

When Mitch began his explanation, there were remnants of fear in his voice, and his voice was modest, but it soon changed. It became almost giddy. "I was out riding my grandpa's bike and I saw this dog sort of running loose," he told them. "I recognized him from seeing him in your yard. So I, you know, thought I should bring him home to you."

Nothing he'd said yet was an outright lie, although it seemed to part of him that lying was precisely what he was doing.

"He let me get close enough to see that the name on his tag was Jasper, and so I just called him and he came with me." He paused briefly, then blurted out, "And he's *fast*! I barely pedaled some of the way back, he was running so hard. He seems like a great dog. A really great dog . . ."

"Slow down," said Papa Carl, straightening his bent shoulders and moving his hands about as if he were shooing a low-flying bug or waving at his feet.

Mitch shook his head and blinked. He was exhausted—physically and emotionally.

The intruder father said thank you and said that his name was Peter and said what his wife's and children's names were and extended his hand to shake Mitch's and said thank you once more.

All the intruders thanked him. But it was the girl, Lolly, who thanked him the most.

"It was my fault Jasper got away," said Lolly.

"Yeah, look," said the boy named Spencer. "The hook works just fine." He held up the latch at the end of the leash, nearly touching Lolly's nose.

He opened and closed the latch, probably a dozen times.

"Don't rub it in," she said to her brother behind a cupped hand, but loud enough for Mitch to hear.

"I forgot to hook Jasper to the tree rightly," she explained, turning toward Mitch. "So you saved my life. Thank you, thank you, thank you." Her eyes gleamed. She rushed toward Mitch and hugged him.

"It's okay," he said, shrinking away from her. "I didn't really do anything." But he *had* done something. And he felt guilty that Lolly had been blamed for that something. He tried, and managed, to push the heavy feeling aside, though, because everyone was being so nice to him, so welcoming. Already he felt pulled—from one life into another.

"Do you want to stay for lunch?" asked Spencer. "If it's okay."

"It's okay," said his mother.

"We have to wash Jasper first," said Lolly. "He stinks."

Mitch looked to Papa Carl.

Papa Carl nodded.

"We can swim after we eat," said Spencer.

"Or play one of those old board games in the closet," said Lolly. "Or play with our long-lost dog."

"Okay," Mitch replied, smiling. "Yes."

It was toward the bright middle of the day, and for the first time in a long, long while, Mitch was happy.

They washed the dog and ate lunch outside and played an old board game and swam. Mitch and Spencer tossed Mitch's football back and forth and threw rocks into the lake and swam again.

Lolly was either right with the boys or close by, watching, listening. Jasper was always nearby, too.

The air around Mitch—the world—had softened. Gone were the sharp edges and pointy corners of the past weeks.

How long would it last?

## 8 ● SPENCER

"He's a charming young man," said Lolly. "Absolutely charming." She scurried across the kitchen and daintily put her dirty breakfast dishes in the sink. "His name is Mitch Sinclair. He's twelve years old. He's got the blackest hair I ever saw."

She seemed to Spencer as if she were an actress on a stage giving a performance as Birdy Lake—or was it Mrs. Mincebottom?—speaking not to any one real person, but to an invisible audience, a full house. And because he was in such a good mood, she wasn't annoying him at all. Spencer was happy because he'd made a new friend.

It was two days after Mitch Sinclair had found Jasper and returned him. Spencer and Mitch had spent that afternoon together, and the next day, yesterday, as well.

He and Mitch had no plan for today, other than that expressed in their parting words the night before. "See you tomorrow," Spencer had said. "I'll come over as early as I can," Mitch had replied.

Spencer looked out the window toward Mitch's grandparents' house. He squinted at the lilacs, trying to see through them. No sign of Mitch.

Heavy gray clouds were blotting out the sun. There was a distinct feel and smell to the morning. He guessed that rain would soon set in.

Lolly continued to babble as she rearranged the cereal boxes on the counter. "We had a perfectly delightful time yesterday."

Yesterday. Mitch had been with Spencer's family nearly every waking moment. Most of the day had been taken up with swimming and just hanging out.

When Spencer and Mitch played catch with

Mitch's football, Spencer was impressed with how hard Mitch could throw. A couple of passes in particular were so like bullets they stung, and there was no way Spencer could hold on to them.

"I hope I can throw like you someday," Spencer had yelled. He took his time chasing down the missed balls, stalling to shake the pain out of his hand.

"Sorry," Mitch would shout. He eased up after a while, tossing soft, high-arcing lobs more than anything else.

When Spencer had caught several in a row, Mitch said, "Good job!"

Spencer smiled confidently. "Thanks!"

They talked about going fishing but never got around to it. They discussed building a raft; they never got around to this, either.

They climbed the maple tree in Spencer's yard, which made Spencer think of Jasper. "I'm really glad you found Jasper," he said as he settled into a nice, comfortable crook.

"Yeah. No problem," Mitch replied quickly and

sharply. Surprisingly, and for no apparent reason, he jumped down from the tree right then, landing with a solid thud, even though they'd just climbed up. He started walking away.

Spencer was confused. Mitch had reacted almost as if his, Spencer's, comment had been some sort of slight or insult, rather than an expression of gratitude. Spencer hung from the lowest branch and dropped to the ground. He jogged to catch up with Mitch. "You all right?" he asked.

"Yeah," Mitch grunted. "Of course. Let's swim some more."

"Okay. I have to tell my mom, though."

"Why do you always have to tell your mom if you go in the lake?"

Spencer hesitated. He had been feeling more grown-up and important than usual; being with a twelve-year-old had done this to him. But Mitch's question was draining him of the feeling. At home, his best friends were mostly nine or ten, and the twelve-year-olds he knew in the neighborhood were too cool for him, barely noticed him any longer. "Oh, she's just a worrier," he decided to say, in as offhand a manner as possible.

At one point in the afternoon, when they were swimming, a round of Marco Polo that included Lolly morphed into a loud, silly romp, complete with splashing and dunking of one another and theatrical flailing about.

"Careful!" Spencer's mother cautioned from the shore. Her voice carried easily across the water and seemed to have come from a loudspeaker. She was always there, a constant, keeping tabs on anyone in the lake.

The one-word warning put a damper on their rowdiness. The three of them grew quiet. Their arms returned to their sides like umbrellas closing.

Spencer slapped at the water, then trailed his fingers through it. He fastened his eyes on the snake-like ripples he'd created, wondering what to say.

"My brother drowned," said Lolly. "A long, long time ago, before I was even born." She said this with some importance, but in her own voice.

Spencer nodded. "I was two. He was four. I don't even remember it."

Mitch offered a jerky tip of his head. "Oh," he said softly. "Sorry." His eyes traveled around. Water. Sky. Hands. Sky. Water.

"That's why my mom's watching us," said Spencer. He needed to say this, and felt better having done so.

A sympathetic "mmm . . . mmm" escaped from Mitch's closed lips. And then he said, "My parents are getting divorced." He shrugged.

Now it was Spencer's turn to say sorry. He chewed on his lower lip and stared at the reflection of the bright blue sky that surrounded him. Concentrating. There were so many wrinkles on the surface of the lake it looked like a bedsheet in the morning. Spencer couldn't imagine his parents getting divorced. That seemed worse to him than the death of a brother you didn't remember.

"At school last year my teacher was divorced,"

said Lolly. "But she has a new friend now—she told us. And she got to keep her dog." Lolly turned a circle. Her ears stuck out of her slicked-down hair like pale half-moons. "If we ever got divorced, I'd get to keep Jasper."

This was a ridiculous statement, and yet Spencer said, "No, *I* would."

"Jasper likes me better," said Lolly.

"That is such a lie," said Spencer. He splashed his sister. Right in the face.

She splashed him back. Then Mitch splashed both of them. In no time at all, they were wrapped up in another boisterous game, and Spencer was laughing so hard he'd temporarily forgotten about his mother keeping watch on shore.

"It's getting darker and darker," said Lolly, now folding and unfolding a dish towel in a fretful manner. "I hope the dear boy gets here soon."

A disturbance arose. The low clouds moved fast, like rolling clumps of steel wool. Lightning flashed.

Thunder rumbled. The wind flared up, stirring the trees. Next, a downpour. And then a brisk rapping on the front door.

Spencer saw Mitch through the window, and saw Mitch's mother, too, lagging behind him, gripping a lavender flower-patterned umbrella. The umbrella seemed to have a mind of its own, pulling this way and that way, shooting up, then dropping dramatically and holding steady.

Spencer ran to the door and opened it. "I was waiting for you," he said.

"*We* were waiting," said Lolly.

Mitch's mother left her umbrella outside and followed Mitch in, "Wipe your shoes, honey," she whispered loudly over the drumming of the rain.

Mitch shuffled his feet hurriedly across the doormat and nodded beyond his shoulder. "This is my mom. Oh, yeah, duh, you met her the other day."

Their meeting had been very brief. Mitch had scooted Spencer away from his mother so quickly that Spencer had barely noticed her.

Spencer and Lolly said hello.

"Mitch has been over here a lot the last two days, so I came to see if you'd like to play at our house. Mitch's grandparents' house."

Mitch cringed. "When you say 'play' like that, it sounds like you're talking about two-year-olds." He scowled at her.

"I'm sorry," Mitch's mother said gravely. She dipped her chin toward Spencer, away from Mitch, and blinked. Was she embarrassed? Being apologetic?

"I'd rather stay here," said Mitch.

She smiled—a tolerant and rueful smile. "Okay. Sure. But I want to check with Spencer's parents." She glanced around, still smiling, but now the smile seemed forced and fixed to Spencer, like the mouth on a statue. "It's a nice house," she said.

"It was my grandparents'," said Spencer.

"And now it's ours," said Lolly in singsong.

Spencer's parents entered the room and invited Mitch's mother to stay for coffee or tea.

"I'd like that," Spencer heard her say.

Spencer led Mitch out to the screened porch. Lolly joined them, but Jasper wouldn't. He remained in the kitchen, squeezed into the small space between the stove and the refrigerator, riding out the weather.

"We'd be drenched out there," said Spencer.

"Soaked," said Mitch.

"You're sort of soaked already," said Lolly. "Your shirt's like a map of the world."

Mitch looked downward at the huge wet areas darkening his T-shirt. "Yeah." He grabbed the shirt by its hem and waved it. He fanned it about as if it were on fire.

"It'll dry," said Lolly. She raised one eyebrow and wiggled it (something Spencer repeatedly tried to do, but couldn't). "I see your belly button. Now I don't. Now I do. Now I don't. . . ."

Mitch let go of his shirt and ran his hands one after the other through his hair. "You're funny," he said to Lolly in a kindly, older-brother sort of way.

"Funny looking, funny sounding, funny acting,

funny smelling," said Spencer. Lolly's remark made him think of performing his belly trick, in which he'd puff out his stomach, big as a watermelon, then suck it in so that you could see his clearly defined ribs over the cave of his chest. His friends at home thought it hilarious, but he decided against it.

Lolly shrugged. "Yesterday you were soaked in sunshine. Today—rain." She giggled.

Spencer rolled his eyes and groaned.

They listened to and watched the storm. They stood close to the screen except when the rain blew in, then they'd jump back, laughing. Raindrops stuck to the screen in places—an unfinished needlepoint stitched in diamonds. One thunderclap was so loud they all gasped and shuddered. The world is cracking open, thought Spencer. The sound was penetrating. He could feel it inside his body for a second, like an extra pulse. He was glad he wasn't alone. He was glad he could hear the rise and fall of his parents' voices in the next room.

After a while, Mitch's mother came out to the

porch and said, "It's fine for you to stay, but I'd love to have you all at our house later."

"Yeah, yeah, yeah," Mitch mumbled.

When the rain let up and the sun broke through the clouds, they went outside. It was clear and light, and everything glistened. Birds darted and sang. The wind had quieted. It was as if a scrim or backdrop had been lifted. The storm, the heavy cast to the morning, was gone.

"The grass is slippery," said Spencer. He'd discovered this by accident, nearly falling as he'd stepped onto the lawn. Then he ran and slid on purpose, seeing how far he could go.

Mitch slid even farther. "My grandma would kill me if I did this on *her* grass."

"Isn't there supposed to be a rainbow?" asked Lolly.

"I don't see one," said Spencer.

"Me neither," said Mitch.

Near the lilacs, Spencer spied Mitch's football.

He ran and slid, ran and slid, in that direction. He scooped up the football. "Do you want to play?" he asked.

"Yeah."

"I hate football," Lolly announced. "And I don't even care about F.M.S." Then she said something about a lost rainbow and scuttled indoors.

"What's F.M.S.?" asked Mitch.

"It stands for 'fear of missing something,'" Spencer explained. "Just a dumb family thing." With Lolly gone, he felt a certain sense of freedom. "She's sort of annoying," he said, approaching Mitch. He handed him the football.

Mitch responded with a shrug and a crooked smile. He motioned for Spencer to move, to increase the distance between them. "You can go uphill, so it'll be easier for you to throw. Here."

The ball sailed back and forth between them. Like a little zeppelin, thought Spencer. They got a nice rhythm flowing. Spencer started keeping track, silently, of the number of passes he'd caught.

"Go deep," Mitch called.

Spencer jogged backward a few steps.

"Deeper!"

Spencer turned and ran, making a large, sweeping arc. The ball was above him, ahead of him. He sprinted, extending his arms as far as he could. He wanted to catch the football so badly. He wanted to impress Mitch.

His fingers touched the ball—he had it—but he slipped on the soggy grass, lost his balance, and fell. The ball popped from his grasp and tumbled down the sloping yard toward Mitch.

"Nice try." Mitch picked up the football and came to Spencer. "You okay?"

Spencer's cheeks burned. "Yeah," he said. He flexed his toes, realizing how wet his shoes were—straight through to his socks. "I'm so bad."

"No, you're not. The sun was probably in your eyes."

"A baby could have caught that."

Mitch turned Spencer's comments into a game.

"I'm so bad, I couldn't catch a cold at the North Pole in a swimming suit." He fumbled comically with the football and dropped it, obviously on purpose.

Spencer tried to laugh. It sounded like snorting. "I'm so bad—" he began. If only he could come up with something good enough, clever enough, so that Mitch would think he was funny. He finally said, "I'm so bad, I wear brown-stained Hello Kitty underwear and pee in my bed every night." It was something he'd heard someone say at school once.

"I'm so bad," said Mitch, "I make candles out of my own earwax."

They both laughed. Then it was quiet.

"Who's your favorite team?" Mitch asked. "The Packers?"

"Actually, the Bears."

"The Bears?"

"Yeah," said Spencer. "Because my dad is a Bear fan. He grew up in Chicago."

"My dad," said Mitch. A long pause. "Isn't." It appeared as if he were talking more to himself than to

Spencer. When he stopped, his mouth hung open like that on a broken toy. He seemed sad or mad or both. Something.

Spencer wished that he could bring the good mood back. "You want to hear something weird?" he asked. He was taking a risk. Confiding was always a risk.

Mitch nodded vigorously, as if he were eager to change the subject from his father to anything else.

"I think there's a ghost at our house," said Spencer, tilting his head to one side and speaking in a most serious tone.

He went on, telling Mitch about the goggles in the birdbath in long, fast, run-on sentences, barely taking time to inhale, barely noticing the complicated looks crossing Mitch's face. "But the freakiest was this pile of sugar, or something, by the front door—and I was the only one who saw it—and I know it could only be from Matty—that's my brother—because it had a number twelve drawn into it—and he'd be twelve if he were alive—and a turtle was drawn into it, too, and a turtle is sort of his symbol because—"

"That was supposed to be a soccer ball, not a tur—"

Silence.

"I'm not a very good artist. . . ." Mitch's voice thinned to a whisper.

The air was hot, growing hotter, and, thought Spencer, crackling with meanness. Closing in. They had been walking in circles, the circles becoming smaller. Now they stood still, held in suspension, near the lake in the glaring sun. Would they ever speak to each other again?

Bewildered and angry, Spencer snatched the football from Mitch's hands, backed up, and drilled it at him as hard as he could. He wanted to crack Mitch's ribs. He wanted to smash him into a million pieces.

The ball grazed Mitch's leg and bounced into the lake. "Hey!" said Mitch.

"Hey yourself," said Spencer. He felt tricked. And ashamed that he'd been tricked.

Mitch waded into the water without bothering to

take off his shoes, retrieved the football, and whipped it at Spencer. Spencer caught it, right in his gut. He folded over it, feeling as if he'd been struck by a bomb.

"Did you do anything else?" Spencer asked bitterly when he could breathe again. "What were you going to do next?"

"Nothing."

And then a new thought occurred to Spencer. He intended the words as a challenge, but his voice was shaky and sounded weak, "Did you let Jasper go?"

"I *found* him, remember?" said Mitch, squinting his eyes and averting them.

"Yeah." Spencer swayed, shifting his weight from foot to foot. "I know."

Birds twittered loudly, like an audience gossiping about them. The sun was a ball of fire. A fine sheen of sweat covered Spencer's arms and legs. His throat felt rough.

"I didn't mean anything bad," Mitch told him. "I didn't even know you. Or anything about you or your brother." His hair hung over his forehead and into his eyes like a black glove. He flipped his hair aside and looked directly at Spencer. "I would never have done it if I'd known you."

Cautiously Spencer tossed the football to Mitch. Mitch caught it and gently lobbed it back. Again. Again.

Spencer cocked his arm to throw, continuing their exchange, but hesitated. He tapped his teeth together, thinking. "But," he said, "I still don't get it. Why? Why did you do it?"

Mitch explained how he'd wanted to live in the house with his mother, before Spencer had arrived. And how he'd wanted to scare away the new people— whoever they might be. He explained how he'd spilled sugar in his grandmother's pantry and needed to get rid of it—that's why the sugar ended up on Spencer's porch. And he explained how after he'd taken the goggles, he'd felt so guilty he'd bundled them around a rock and thrown them back toward Spencer's house in an attempt to return them as fast as possible without being seen.

"Why did you draw a soccer ball and a twelve in the sugar?" asked Spencer.

"The twelve because I'm twelve," Mitch answered. "And the soccer ball because it's all I could think of. It was just random. All of it was random."

It's strange, Spencer reflected, how the same simple thing could be interpreted so differently. What Mitch had meant to be a soccer ball, he, Spencer, had been positive was a turtle. Matty's turtle.

"Why is a turtle a sign for your brother anyway?" asked Mitch.

"Because he swallowed a little turtle statue when he was a baby and pooped it out. We keep the turtle on our mantel."

"Oh," said Mitch, nodding. He drew himself up, his shoulders nearly touching his ears. Then he sighed heavily and said, "Come here."

He showed Spencer the dark, hidden place he'd made for himself under the porch. "Watch your head," he told Spencer. "It stays pretty cool in here." Once Spencer was well within the grasp of the shadows, Mitch unfastened the photograph of his family he'd taped to the ceiling. "This is my dad," he said, pointing. "*Was* my dad." He ripped the photo in half, ripped it twice more, and jammed the pieces into his pocket. "I was under here the night you came. I was so scared. Jasper smelled me and I thought he'd give me away. Or bite me."

"Jasper would never bite anyone," said Spencer.

"I know that now, but that night I didn't." He yawned. "Let's get out of here."

As they crawled out into the light, Mitch said, "I didn't hurt anyone. I didn't break anything. I didn't abandon anyone."

Spencer knew that Mitch was referring to his father.

"I never would have done it if I'd known you," Mitch repeated.

They dillydallied around the border of the yard. Silently, Spencer recalled how he'd sensed he was being watched that first night at the lake. Things were coming into clear focus. Spencer could feel his body relax. The anger faded away and was replaced by a wave of relief that buoyed him.

It didn't happen all at once, but before they'd completed one full circle, Spencer knew some things. Deeply. He knew that there was no ghost. He knew that Mitch hadn't meant to do anything mean to him, to make fun of him. And he knew that he wanted to keep the house at Bird Lake more than ever.

"So there's no ghost," said Spencer. He sounded almost jolly, the relief lightening his voice.

"No ghost," said Mitch.

After a few quiet moments passed, Spencer asked, "Are you hungry? Do you want to have lunch?"

Spencer was glad that he hadn't told his parents or Lolly about the ghost. And he knew he wouldn't tell them about what had happened with Mitch, either. He'd squirrel away this information, this piece of his life. Keeping it private. A secret. As he became older, he was doing this more and more.

He saw and heard something else that day that he would squirrel away.

It was late. Night. He couldn't sleep, and he'd heard voices, so he crept downstairs. All the lights were off. The narrow hallway that led to the kitchen had no windows and was so dark he groped along, taking small steps to avoid stumbling. This is what it must feel like, he thought, to be at the bottom of the lake at the deepest part at midnight. As he entered the kitchen, the voices became more distinct. His parents were talking, out on the screened porch. His mother sounded as if she were crying.

The moon, already starting to recede on its right side, was blotchy but bright against the obsidian sky. It provided enough illumination so that Spencer could identify outlines, shapes. He pressed himself against the refrigerator and angled his head until he could see his parents.

His mother said, "I just don't know. I don't know if I can stay here. I really wanted to. You know how much I used to love this place."

His father said, "Do you want to go home tomorrow?"

"I don't know. Maybe."

"Let's see how you feel in the morning."

Spencer heard something fall and clatter across the floor. It had to be something small, because the noise it made was small. He saw his mother bend to pick the thing up.

It was the little turtle. He was certain.

He left, quietly moving through the house and back to bed. Parents have secrets, too, he thought. He'd never known exactly how Matty had drowned, what had actually happened. Was it someone's fault? He didn't want to know. Ever.

Maybe some things are worse than ghosts, he thought.

## 9 • MITCH

Mitch's night was marked by fitful, shallow sleep. In the morning, the dream from which he awoke left him ragged. The dream—the fragment he could remember—had been ordinary but turned surreal.

In it, he and Spencer were swimming in the lake on a sunny day. With jarring abruptness, the sky darkened to an eerie silver, the full moon rose, and Spencer was the size of a giant. Wielding a dip net, he lumbered after Mitch, bellowing, "Where's my dog? Where's my dog?" He swiped at Mitch, creating monumental waves and high winds. Reflected light from the moon danced upon the surface of the churning water like blinding, dazzling stars cast down from above. Just as the net lowered over Mitch, he emerged from sleep with a start.

Trying to shake the dream, Mitch quickly got out of bed and pulled on his clothes. He trudged through the house to the kitchen window like an old man.

In the east, the sky was pink, but the top of the sky was still a deep, smoky blue. Mitch didn't need to check a clock or a watch to know that it was early, very early, and yet lights were already on at Spencer's house. Many of the windows were aglow—yellow, unblinking jack-o'-lantern eyes staring down the dawn.

From upstairs came the sound of footfalls. Cherry? He didn't feel like talking to anyone, so he went outside, to the lake. Without a jacket or shoes on, the morning chill and the cold, dewy grass made him shiver. Clumps of gray-brown foam lapped at the shore, reminding him of some piece of his dream, but the dream was slipping away.

Would it be rude to go to Spencer's house this

early? he wondered. The lights were beckoning, and yet something held him back.

He yawned. Not a soul was around. He was entirely alone. That the truth had come out yesterday had been a relief, but the issue of unhooking Jasper's leash still hung over him. Poor Lolly, blamed for something she hadn't done, and the real culprit deemed a hero. When Spencer had questioned him about Jasper, Mitch's heart had pounded, taking over his chest. And, too, there were his initials he'd carved into the front-porch railing. He hoped that they hadn't been discovered. He didn't know how to deal with this either. And to make matters worse, by carving his initials he'd implicated himself. Stupid.

Shut your mind, he told himself. Snap it tight.

A door creaked in the near distance. A noisy spring expanded and compressed. Recognizing the sounds, Mitch turned to look at Spencer's house. Jasper trotted out into the yard, disappeared behind a bush, then trotted back inside. Taking this as a signal, Mitch walked to Spencer's.

As he mounted the steps Mitch was tempted to bend low and steal a peek at his initials. But he didn't. He knocked softly on the door and stepped back and off to the side. He heard Jasper bark, but Spencer's father answered the door alone.

"Good morning, Mitch," said Spencer's father.

"Hi. Can Spencer play football or swim or something?"

"He can't right now." Another series of barks from Jasper. "You're up early."

"I saw lights," said Mitch, "so I thought it was okay to come over."

"Oh, we're all up." Then with a noticeable drop to his voice, he said, "We're having a family meeting right now."

Suddenly Mitch became wary. Because of me? he wondered. Had Spencer told his parents about yesterday? Was that what they were meeting about? "Oh," he said, blinking rapidly.

"I'll have him stop over when we're done."

"Okay."

Spencer's father nodded. There was a grim set to his mouth.

Without meaning to or realizing it, Mitch nodded in return, mirroring the expression.

Mitch was off the stoop in one long, quick stride. He roamed the yard, working his way home. To him, a family meeting always meant something bad: a discussion of unacceptable grades or new chores, or the announcement of a canceled vacation. A disappointment that, in his parents' view, needed an official setting in which to be presented.

He decided to eat breakfast and wait for Spencer. Maybe they could go to the public beach today. Or to the general store. Or to—

Another piece of his dream flashed to the surface of his awareness. Something was looming above him, closing in. A mesh cage? The net. In a nanosecond, the odd sensation had vanished. He looked over his shoulder. Here and gone in the blink of an eye.

● ● ●

His mother was waiting when he entered the kitchen. "Pancakes?" she asked. On the counter, which was dusted with flour and gave the impression that a miniature snow squall had blustered through, stood a bowl of batter. The griddle was on the stove, ready. A bottle of maple syrup was on the table, opened.

"Sure. Thanks. Where are Papa Carl and Cherry?"

"Cherry's in the basement doing laundry. She declined my offer of pancakes. And as far as I know, Papa Carl's still in bed."

Mitch sat at the table. He loved pancakes and chewed his lower lip in anticipation. The kitchen soon filled with good, warm smells.

"We're going to Madison today to look at apartments," his mother said as she checked the underside of a pancake with a spatula. "You and I." She kept her head bent, her attention focused on her task, and if Mitch hadn't known better, he might have thought that she was talking to the stove.

"Do I have to go?" he asked in a low voice.

Batter sizzled. Waves of heat and steam rose between mother and son, marbling a shaft of sunlight. The clock on the wall ticked in judgment—*tsk, tsk, tsk.*

She took a moment to compose herself, it seemed, turning away before turning back and saying, "Yes." She smiled blandly, holding the spatula the stiff way a crossing guard holds a stop sign. "It'll be your home, too. I want you to help choose it."

His intent was not to make her angry or to irritate her. And the implications of what she was proposing hadn't sunk in. He just wanted to stay at Bird Lake. "Okay," he replied, resigned. "But when will we get back?"

"I don't know. What's the rush?"

Mitch shrugged. He watched her flip pancakes and stack them on a plate and carry the plate over to him. "Thanks," he said.

"You're welcome."

"Aren't you eating?" he asked.

"I'm not very hungry. My breakfast," she said,

picking up her coffee mug from the counter and rais-
ing it as if she was toasting him.

After a few bites, he said, "They're good."

"Good."

"Do you think we'll be back in the late afternoon?
Before dark? I wanted to hang out with Spencer."

"I don't know." Her voice had become icy. She
tossed some silverware into the sink. The silverware
clattered and clinked, speaking for her, words he
imagined her thinking: You frustrate me.

After a weighty silence, she said, "One of the
apartments has a pool." Her voice had been trans-
formed, had become the equivalent of tiptoeing. "I
thought that might be nice for you."

Within twenty minutes, Mitch and his mother
were in their car en route to Madison. As the car
lurched from the driveway onto the road, Mitch saw
that Spencer's family's kayak was leaning against their
car. His heart fell. They're going to have fun today, he
thought. Without me.

● ● ●

Mitch's mother signed a lease for the first apartment they looked at, the one with a swimming pool. It wasn't far from Mitch's old house, so he'd go to the same school as last year. They could move in on August fifteenth, which gave them time to work at getting the house ready to sell.

"Dad will help, right?" asked Mitch.

"Yes," his mother replied. Then she quickly changed the subject. "I like it. Do you like it?"

"It's okay." Mitch was slumped in the backseat of the car. They were driving away from the apartment complex, weaving through blanched, orderly streets he'd traveled on hundreds of times before.

"I need to check on a few things at home," his mother said, glancing over her shoulder toward him.

Mitch didn't want to go into the house, and the closer they came to it, the lower he slumped. He didn't want to see anyone he knew. "I'll wait in the car," he told her.

His mother steered the car into the driveway and turned off the engine. "Is there anything you'd like me to get for you inside?"

"Nah."

"Why don't you run over to Aaron's or Sam's? That might cheer you up, I'm sure they'd be happy to see you."

"No."

"They know about Dad and me. They'd like to see you."

He straightened up a little. "I don't want to see anyone."

"Okay. I just want us to get back to normal as soon as possible. The longer you . . . we . . . avoid things, the harder it will be."

Absently, Mitch unbuckled his seat belt and toyed with it, moving the silver latch so that it glinted and, in turn, projected a white, elongated star onto his mother's hair. He felt an undercurrent of muted sadness encroaching upon and controlling the day.

The rearview mirror connected them—it was where their eyes met. His mother's eyes widened when she said, "Will you talk to me? You can tell me anything, you know."

Mitch shrugged. "I don't feel like talking."

"Okay. I understand." She smiled gently and kissed the air. "Inarticulateness," she said with no emotion in her voice, "is the language of men and boys." She opened the car door.

"What's that mean?" asked Mitch.

"Nothing." The door closed quietly.

Yawning, Mitch lay facedown in a rectangle of hot sun, his arms folded into a pretzel, his head buried in the upholstery. He pictured Spencer and his father driving to the public boat landing and paddling their kayak around the end of the lake by the general store and the library.

Slowly Mitch lifted his head and stared at the house. It looked the same and different at once. He wondered if it smelled the same. When they'd come home from a trip, the familiar smell would greet them, a genuine presence as they walked into the front hallway. He'd been away from the house for longer periods of time than this, although it seemed the longest.

When his mother returned, she was carrying a

stack of file folders and an overflowing canvas bag. She placed the items in the trunk and got into the car. "Are you hungry?" she asked. "It's lunchtime."

"Sort of."

"You can pick where we go. We can go to State Street or to the food court at the mall. Anywhere you like."

"Let's just go to a fast-food place on the highway. That way we'll get back sooner."

So that's what they did.

The only real bright spot for Mitch that entire morning and afternoon came after lunch, when they stopped for gas. "Here," said his mother, slipping both a twenty-dollar bill and a five-dollar bill into his hand. "Go pay for the gas, please. I'm getting twenty dollars' worth. Use the five to get a snack for the drive to the lake."

Mitch scanned the racks of candy and salty snacks. He decided on a pack of gum, which would leave him with money to spare, and so he continued to survey the possibilities. As he picked up a bag of potato chips, a small section of dog and cat food caught his attention. If he didn't buy anything else, he'd have enough money to buy a small box of dog biscuits for Jasper. His mood lightened as he made his final decision. He paid the cashier and ran to the car.

"You look happy," said his mother. "What did you get?"

Smiling, he held up the dog biscuits.

"Oh, great. This is what we've come to," she said. She laughed, and he knew she was joking.

"They're for Jasper," he told her.

"I figured as much." A pause. "You're a nice boy."

He smiled again. He was doing a good thing, and he knew it. Periodically on the way home, he shook the box to match the tempo of the music playing on the radio.

"You're a nice boy," said his mother, "and a funny one."

"Yes, I am," he replied. "Yes, I am."

Mitch hurried from the car right to Spencer's house. The late-afternoon sun remained a force, a great white ornament dangling above the treetops. Already he knew, as he knocked on the door. The first clue: no barking. More evidence came to him like still images flashing across a screen. No open windows. No swimming suits and towels left on the bushes to dry. No kayak. No car. No canoe in the middle of the yard. No dog dish under the maple tree. No folding chairs on the lawn.

The house was closed up and locked. They were gone.

Knowing it was pointless, he ran around the house to check the screened porch. It was orderly and clean, and looked officially abandoned. In sadness, anger, and frustration, he shook the box of dog biscuits at the little house. And he glared at it, as if it were a person who had betrayed him.

From beyond the lilacs he heard Cherry calling his name. He kicked the ground savagely and followed her voice.

She was at the bottom of the porch steps, drying her hands in a dish towel. "Your friend came by looking for you," she said. "The little girl, too. Three times. The last time he said to tell you good-bye."

"How long ago?" Mitch asked.

"Oh, several hours, I'd guess. Before lunch."

"What else did he say?"

"Well, he wanted to know if you'd be here for the rest of the summer. I told him I couldn't be certain. He thought he'd be coming back at some time."

"When?"

"He didn't say."

Mitch tried to remember the street name on Jasper's tag, but couldn't.

As if she somehow had access to and understood the train of Mitch's thoughts, Cherry said, "I wrote down our address and phone number here at the lake and gave it to him. I told him to let us know when he'd be back."

"Thank you."

"I thought you'd like that."

"Did he give you his address or phone number?"

"No. No, he didn't."

"Oh."

"I did my best." Her hands moved uneasily, awkwardly, around and around the dish towel.

"Thank you, Cherry."

The beginnings of a smile quickly rose on her lips, then collapsed just as quickly. "I've got some cooking to finish," she said.

Mitch's eyes strayed, then fixed on her dish towel. "I'll help you," he said.

"That's okay," said Cherry.

A spell of silence descended upon them. They went their separate ways—Cherry inside the house, Mitch down to the lake.

There was a particular rock by the shore—large, smooth, and mottled—where Mitch had seen his mother sit before. He dropped the box of dog biscuits into the tall grass nearby and hopped onto the rock and got comfortable. He stared ahead, out at the water. Hundreds and hundreds of finely engraved ripples flowed toward him, one after the other, endlessly. His vision blurred. He remembered the last thing he'd done with Spencer. The previous night, he'd played cards, a game called King in the Corner, with Spencer and his family at the rickety table in their cramped kitchen. Because the small room had been bathed in shadow, the dim overhead lamp had been like a dull moon in a cave. Mitch had been happy. So happy that ordinary time had lost its usual hold. He'd truly wanted to win and tried to, but truly didn't care at all if he lost. Laughter, as easy and natural as breathing, had come and gone in surges.

Mitch heard something and jerked his head around.

"It's just me," said his mother. "Cherry told me about Spencer. I'm sorry you missed him."

"It's okay." He made room for her on the rock.

"Hang on to those dog biscuits. I'm sure they'll be back."

Mitch could feel his mother searching his face. He wondered what she was looking for.

A car sped past on the main road. Mitch turned, listening until the sound of the car faded away.

"I'm going in to help Cherry with dinner, whether she likes it or not. I'll call you when it's ready."

"Can we play a card game after dinner? All of us? It's called King in the Corner. I'll teach it to you."

"I'd love to," his mother said. "But I can't speak for your grandparents. I can only speak for myself." She slid off the rock to leave. "Don't forget the dog biscuits," she said. She tossed her hand and fluttered her fingers—part salute, part wave, part blown kiss.

After dinner, Papa Carl went to the store for coffee for the next morning, Cherry insisted on weeding a section of her garden before nightfall, and Mitch's mother received a lengthy phone call that drew her into the spare bedroom with the door closed behind her.

Mitch wondered if they'd ever play cards. He sat on the front steps. Darkness was settling over everything like fog; Cherry wouldn't be able to work much longer. Hunched, she inched slowly along the rows of flowers, bringing to mind the image of a dusky animal scavenging for food. In the dwindling light, Spencer's house was a lifeless gray box. It seemed silly to Mitch that he'd believed he'd actually live there. I'm moving to an apartment, he thought. This was a fact now. A fact of his life. Tears leaked from his smarting eyes.

Blinking, he looked for the moon. It was nowhere to be seen. A few nights ago it had been full, attention-seeking, a glorious advertisement for itself. Now it was concealed behind clouds. But it was still there. Somewhere.

Just because you can't see something doesn't mean it isn't there.

Headlights illuminated the velvety yard, heralding Papa Carl's return. It took him a minute to maneuver his knees out of his truck. He walked stiffly, carrying a small bag in the crook of one arm like an infant. "My coffee," he said.

"Yep," Mitch replied.

"Are you ready to teach us that card game, Mr. Mitch?" asked Papa Carl.

"You bet."

"Me, too. Go find your mother. I'll round up Cherry."

"Okay," said Mitch. He rose and walked into the quiet house. For a moment he felt—perfectly, completely, particularly—alone.

And then Papa Carl's voice boomed in the night with an urgency that indicated that a statement of pressing importance was being made. "Call it quits and come in, Cherry," he said. "Mitch is going to teach us a thing or two."

## 10 ● SPENCER

"What are you doing?" Spencer asked Lolly.

"I'm trying to remember everything," Lolly answered. "In case we never come back." She was brushing her cheek against the screen on the outside of the porch. Her eyes were closed.

"We're coming back," said Spencer. "They said we'd come back."

Lolly shrugged.

"I told Mitch's grandma we'd be back."

"She's crabby," said Lolly. "Mrs. Burden."

Spencer agreed. They'd gone to Mitch's house three times looking for Mitch. The last time Mitch's grandmother had gone so far as to say, "You don't have to stop by anymore. I'll send Mitch over when he returns. I doubt it'll be soon. He and his mother are apartment hunting in Madison." Displeasure and distraction had laced her tone and manner. Knowing that he was too timid to try again, and that they'd be departing shortly anyway, Spencer had told her good-bye. She'd written her address and phone number on a slip of paper. "Here," she'd said, extending a wrinkled hand, offering the information. "Call or write to let us know when you're coming to Bird Lake again."

Spencer continued to watch for Mitch's mother's burgundy car. Only if he saw the car would he risk another interaction with Mitch's grandmother. The slip of paper was folded, secure in his pocket.

When Lolly was done with the screen, she dabbled with her fingers in the birdbath, sniffed the bark of the maple tree, and counted the number of pine trees on the side of the house. "Remember, remember," she murmured.

Spencer followed her, observing. "Who are

you today? Birdy Freak Show Lake?"

"I am me," Lolly replied in a measured voice. Her behavior was strange, but, at the same time, she seemed more grown-up than ever to Spencer.

She'd seemed oddly grown-up at their family meeting, too. When Spencer's mother had said that they'd be leaving Bird Lake as soon as they could clean the house and pack, Lolly had appeared unfazed, nodding thoughtfully like an adult. "I understand," she'd said.

Spencer, on the other hand, had had to work hard to keep from crying. The salt and pepper shakers on the table on which he'd been focusing had wavered because of the tears collecting in his eyes. And he'd felt angry, too. He'd taken the spoon he'd been using for his cereal, and under the table he'd gripped it so fiercely with both hands, he'd bent it.

"It's too hard for me to be here because of what happened to Matty," his mother had said. "I suppose part of me knew that all along, but I needed to come out here one more time, just to be sure."

"So you don't like it here at all?" Spencer had asked bravely.

"It's hard to describe," she replied. "I still love it—and I hate it."

"You're not going to sell the house, are you?"

"We'll see," said Spencer's father. "We're not making any decisions like that today."

Spencer peered at his father with imploring eyes.

"One possibility is to rent the house," his father said. "That way we can keep it in the family. Who knows? Maybe one day, when you're an old white-haired man, you'll be sitting right here with your grandchildren."

"I'm never getting married," Spencer said, suddenly annoyed. "But anyway, can I come back this summer? Just for a few days, even? I never got to go fishing. I could see Mitch."

Spencer's father looked questioningly at Spencer's mother. "Well," he said eventually, "if we decide to rent the house, I'll have a lot of fixing up to do. So you can come with me."

"Promise?"

"Promise."

"Even if you don't fix things up? Can we come back?"

Spencer's father's response was not immediate, but it was the response Spencer hoped to hear. "Yes. I think we can work something out."

"Me, too?" asked Lolly.

"Sure."

Spencer wanted to be doubly certain. He wanted to hear it from his mother. "So we can come back, Mom?"

"You can." The words were spoken quietly, but they were important, hanging in the air like an echo.

Spencer's father stood and clasped the top of his chair. "I'll do the dishes," he said. "I've already loaded some things into the car and put the kayak by it. All you two need to take care of is getting your own belongings together. Mom and I will take care of everything else. When you're ready, you can go say good-bye to Mitch and just play around the yard.

Whatever you want. It'll take us awhile. And to make up—a little bit—for disappointing you both, we thought we'd stay at some fun resort tonight. We can go to one of those places with a fancy miniature golf course or a water park."

Lolly perked up. "Good idea."

Spencer didn't respond. He was still taking it all in, processing it. Under the table, his fingers were an antsy, confused tangle. He thought he might snap the spoon in two. He wouldn't look at his mother. And he wouldn't and he wouldn't and he wouldn't. And it felt as if the moment had swelled and he had been permanently anchored at the table with his head drooped. And when he finally did look up, his mother's smooth face had crumpled. But then she swiftly composed herself and said in her mild way, "I'm sorry." And he thought to say, "Me, too" and "I love you," but didn't.

And that was how the family meeting had ended.

Spencer could hear his parents working in the house—the opening and closing of drawers and doors, dishes clinking together, the scraping of furniture against the floor. And he could picture Jasper, having sensed that something was going to happen, following them around, ears alert, nose nudging persistently for reassuring pats.

After she had finished counting the pine trees, Lolly circled through the yard to the lilac bushes. She faced the lilacs with outstretched arms and leisurely made her way down the crooked line, trailing her fingers along the twisty, leafy branches and what remained of the brittle flowers.

"Really, what are you doing?" Spencer asked.

"I already told you—I'm remembering."

Still shadowing his sister, Spencer checked on Mitch's car again. Still gone. Earlier, Mitch had come to the door, interrupting the family meeting. But Spencer hadn't seen him. He wondered if he'd ever see him again.

He thought fleetingly that Mitch and his mother could rent the house, but decided that this was an unrealistic idea. After all, Mitch was looking for an apartment right now. Then Spencer wondered if he and Mitch would ever be friends in Madison. Madison wasn't huge, but big enough that they'd both probably fall into their own routines and never have much to do with each other.

Lolly wheeled about and wandered to the lake. She stood tall at the shore, still as a pole. A gentle breeze ruffled the silver-blue water, and clouds hurried across the sky as if they were going someplace, too.

The morning was large and Spencer was small. These limited minutes at the lake belonged to him, and what did he do with them? He continued to follow Lolly. Next she went to the front porch. She lay down on her back, precisely where Mitch had drawn the soccer ball in sugar. She spread her arms wide into the warming sun. Her hair had fanned out on the wooden planks, forming a halo, one fugitive strand curving across her face like a scar. She looked all around with noteworthy concentration, as if she were absorbing and treasuring every detail of 23 Lakeshore Drive for all time. Her brow would wrinkle slightly, but then an expression of pure tranquillity would return to her face.

Suddenly Lolly's eyes were blazing. "Spencer," she said. She slid closer to the railing and scrutinized its underside. She stiffened. Her placid demeanor had vanished. "Spencer," she said again. "Look."

Spencer came to the railing and crouched. "What?"

She pointed, tracing the letters with her index finger. "M.S.," she whispered. "It's Matty's initials."

The power of the moment was insistent, consuming. A chill fell over Spencer.

But in a few seconds, he knew. "Oh," he said with a broadening smile. "Oh."

M.S. Matty Stone. Mitch Sinclair.

If Spencer had discovered the initials even a day and a half ago, he would have been frightened, just like Lolly.

Lolly had risen to her hands and knees. "What should we do? What does it mean?" She was so excited, her voice was shaking. "Should we tell Mom?"

Briefly, Spencer felt as big as the moon, and full—of secret knowledge and of so many things Lolly was not. He liked the feeling and wanted to hold on to it forever.

But he knew that he would clear things up and calm her down, turn her bewilderment to understanding. Just as he knew that soon they would pile into the car and drive away from Bird Lake.

He also knew that he'd come back again. He knew this as certainly as he knew who had carved the initials into the railing.

"Listen, Lolly," he began, his voice rich and confident. "I can explain everything."

## 11 ● MITCH

June had passed, the Fourth of July was over, and the world hadn't ended.

Mitch had been back to Madison a few times to help his mother get ready for the move to the apartment in August. And he'd reconnected with his friends Aaron and Sam.

Mitch and Cherry had become card buddies. King in the Corner had opened the door to other games—crazy eights, double solitaire, gin. They played several nights a week after dinner.

The next time Mitch had had dinner with his father, the abandoned cell phone had been on the middle of the backseat of the car, no questions asked. Mitch was rarely without it now.

And Mitch had even gone on a picnic and to a fireworks show with his father and his father's girlfriend and lived through it. The woman's name was Torie, although Mitch hadn't called her anything. His mouth could not, would not frame the word: Torie. She didn't have children of her own, which Mitch took as a plus.

"How was she? How was it?" his mother had asked when he'd returned late that night to Bird Lake.

Downwind came the sounds of people celebrating. Small fireworks popped and echoed across the lake. Mitch shrugged. "Okay," he said. Actually, she'd seemed nice enough, but he hadn't wanted to tell his mother.

Despite his apprehension and resistance, life was moving forward. Some things were ending, some were beginning.

He couldn't help but give in to the occasional temptation to replay past events in his mind, altering them, changing them from cruel to comfortable, from sad to happy, from unfair to accommodating. Anything was possible in his imagination. Any ending. If only thinking it could make it so.

Daily, Mitch thought of Spencer and wondered when he'd come back to Bird Lake. Daily, he looked to the empty house for signs of life.

Jasper still weighed heavily on his mind. The guilt worked at him, even in the night. It had become a burden.

The initials he'd carved into the railing had been a burden as well. But those he could easily do something about. One day, late in the afternoon, he gouged at them so that they were no longer legible, doing as little damage as possible to the railing. Before he had finished, something dawned on him. He realized that his initials and Spencer's brother's were the same. It was eerie, an eerie link to Spencer and his family. Maybe, he thought, we were destined to meet and be friends. Or maybe it was just a coincidence.

Mitch was grateful that, as far as he knew, no one

had discovered the initials. If Spencer had stumbled upon them while he believed in Matty's ghost, he would have freaked out. What a stir that would have caused.

During the next week, Mitch sensed that Spencer would soon return. The feeling grew stronger each day. Perhaps that was why the Jasper issue was so unsettling, and the need to resolve it so urgent.

In the middle of July, on what promised to be a beautiful, sunny day, Mitch woke at dawn. Through the window, the trees were charcoal silhouettes against the clearing sky. High above, a handful of fading stars was hanging on. While looking out at it all, Mitch made a decision. He decided that he would write a note to Spencer explaining about Jasper, and apologizing. So many things were beyond his control—especially where his parents were concerned—but this was something he could fix. He didn't know Spencer's address, but if nothing else, he thought that he could slip the note under the front door of the little house with the belief that Spencer would find it at some point.

He got ready. First he turned on the lamp by his bedside. The sudden blast of light was startling. He squinched his eyes and slowly opened them as they adjusted to the brightness. He gathered up a spiral notebook and pen from his backpack, shook the box of dog biscuits (which he'd been keeping on his dresser) for good luck, smoothed his heaped bed-spread, and lay on his stomach diagonally across the mattress.

Stalling, he doodled. He drew a dog and a house the way a young child might. He aimlessly scribbled the word *intruders* and immediately crossed it out. Spencer hadn't been an intruder. If anything, he, Mitch, had been the intruder.

Stalling some more, he chewed on his pen, his fingernail. He remembered his splinter, looked, and realized that it was gone. It had worked itself out without his knowing. Frowning, he examined his finger closely. The only evidence of the splinter that remained was a slight red mark on his skin.

After taking a deep breath, Mitch flipped to a blank page in his notebook. It would be like jumping into the lake first thing in the morning. That inaugural plunge into the water always thrilled him. He wouldn't call it fear, exactly, but something related to it—that feeling when you decide to pitch yourself into the water and anticipate, for a long terrible, wonderful moment, the jolt upon entry. But he would always barrel ahead and do it. He would never chicken out.

The pale blue lines on the paper made him think of ripples on the lake. Already he could feel a lightness inside. He took another deep breath, and he began to write.

## 12 • SPENCER

Inside. The turtle had been back in its usual spot on the mantelpiece for weeks. Out of curiosity, Spencer checked to see if it was still where it belonged. It was. It was such a tiny thing, but now, for Spencer, it meant something big.

Outside. The sky was so blue, clear, and smooth, it looked like blown glass. The warm sunlight poured through Spencer. Excited, he fairly leaped between the house and the car while he waited to leave.

It was mid-July, and Spencer couldn't have been more content. The weather was perfect, the start of school seemed far, far away, and he was going to Bird Lake.

Spencer, his father, and Jasper would spend a few days at the little house. Among other things, they'd loaded fishing gear and a toolbox into the car. The kayak was strapped in place on top.

When he'd known for sure that he'd be going to Bird Lake again, Spencer had decided to call Mitch to tell him. He'd used the number that Mitch's grandmother had given him. It was Mrs. Burden, Cherry, who'd answered the phone. Her sharp, penetrating "Hello?" had surprised Spencer, and his throat had tightened. He did not say a thing, could not utter a sound. Although he'd known that it was impolite to do so, after her third "Hello?" Spencer had hung up. He had Mitch's address and could write him a note, but he'd finally thought that he might as well surprise Mitch. It would be a good surprise.

Spencer's mother had wanted Lolly to stay home with her. At first, Lolly had protested, but after devising a schedule packed with art projects, a picnic with friends, a plan to make ice cream, and a promise to sleep in a tent in the yard one night, she was more than happy not to go.

"I don't even have F.M.S.," Lolly had said to Spencer as he toted his things to the car. "Maybe *you* do."

"I don't," Spencer had replied. He didn't have it at all, not a trace.

"I get to work at the frame shop with Mom, too."

"Uh-huh."

"I get all the scraps of mat board. To keep."

"Good."

Spencer's father wanted to get moving. He'd arranged for a meeting with a carpenter to inspect the house at Bird Lake and discuss needed repairs. "I don't want to be late," said Spencer's father. "Are you ready?"

"Yes," said Spencer. "I'm ready."

After Jasper jumped into the rear of the car, the family huddled together. They hugged. They kissed. Spencer's mother hugged him so tightly and for so long that he thought she might never let go. He squirmed away but then leaned into her and hugged her back as hard as he could.

"I love you," she whispered into his hair.

"Love you, too," he told her quietly.

Earlier in the week, Lolly had bought an old camera at a garage sale for a dollar. It had no film in it. She'd acquired the irritating habit of taking pretend pictures of her parents, Jasper, and Spencer whenever the whim struck her. "Smile," she'd say, pressing the button. She'd brought the camera with her to the car.

"Smile," she said sweetly to Spencer. "Say cheese for Birdy Lake."

Spencer stuck out his tongue and crossed his eyes.

*Click.*

"Perfect, dear," said Lolly.

Spencer and his father slid into the car.

"Wait!" said Lolly. She ran to the house and quickly returned with a piece of paper. "This is for Mitch," she told Spencer, passing the paper to him through the open window.

It was a drawing of Jasper, done with markers. Jasper was tied and padlocked to a tree. The padlock was as big as Jasper. Lolly had drawn the lake in the background, and she'd made the full moon so large that it bled off the page.

"Tell him it's from me," said Lolly. "From Lolly, not Birdy Lake."

"I think he'll know," said Spencer. He flipped the drawing onto the seat beside him.

Lolly poked her head into the car. She was so close to Spencer that he could feel her breath on his face. "Remember everything," she said. "Tell me everything when you get home." Then she stepped back, raised the camera, and aimed it at her brother.

Spencer looked at her—directly at the camera—and smiled nicely for her sake.

*Click.*

He would remember everything. But he might not tell.